YOU'LL
THANK
ME
FOR
THIS

YOU'LL THANK ME FOR THIS

A NOVEL

NINA SIEGAL

MULHOLLAND BOOKS

Little, Brown and Company
New York Boston London

Copyright © 2021 by Hachette Book Group, Inc.

Mulholland Books / Little, Brown and Company
Hachette Book Group
1290 Avenue of the Americas, New York, NY 10104
mulhollandbooks.com

First Edition: March 2021

Mulholland Books is an imprint of Little, Brown and Company, a division of Hachette Book Group, Inc. The Mulholland Books name and logo are trademarks of Hachette Book Group, Inc.

The publisher is not responsible for websites (or their content) that are not owned by the publisher.

The Hachette Speakers Bureau provides a wide range of authors for speaking events. To find out more, go to hachettespeakersbureau.com or call (866) 376-6591.

ISBN 978-0-316-70356-7
LCCN 2020946792

Printing 1, 2021

LSC-C

Printed in the United States of America

To my daughter, Sonia,
and all the girls who are finding their way

I went to the woods because I wished to live deliberately, to front only the essential facts of life, and see if I could not learn what it had to teach, and not, when I came to die, discover that I had not lived.

—Henry David Thoreau

YOU'LL THANK ME FOR THIS

CHAPTER 1

BLINDFOLDED

They handed her a blindfold. She looked at it, turning it over in her hands. It was black, made of a thick fabric, with extra flaps on the sides to make sure no light seeped in at the edges of her vision. It reminded Karin of the blindfolds her mother would wear when they took an international overnight flight from the US back to the Netherlands. She knew that this object would handicap her, taking away her favorite sense, one she relied on pretty heavily. She paused, for just a moment. "Put it on, all of you," he said, with a harsh urgency that startled her. *Goodbye, sight.*

Karin lifted it to her face, pulled the straps over her crown, and instinctively closed her eyes. When she opened them, she tried to see what she could see. It wasn't exactly nothing. There were tiny specks of light, some of them white, some yellowish blue. A little bit of light shining in, like particles of dust. That was it. Had she thought that she'd see shadows or shapes beyond the fabric? Maybe. But no, it was dark enough that she was, essentially, blinded.

After that they all were led by their shoulders to the car, told to step up, to lean forward, to sit back. Confusing instructions when you're still trying to make sense of the blindness. The hands that moved her were rough, not gentle. Hers seemed to be a man's, and he seemed to be in a rush. The hands reached over her body and she could feel his hot breath on her face, hear a little grunting as he pressed her seat belt into its buckle with a resounding click. Then he announced to all of them, "Absolutely no talking," and the doors were slammed shut, *clunk, clunk, clunk.*

She knew that she was in the back seat of a car, not the front, because she could feel the door at her left elbow. What else could she figure out, with her current handicap? She tried to think of it as a game, a sensory experiment, to calm her nerves. And realized that the strongest sensation she had at the moment was the vibration of her own body. Her heart was pounding. She raised a hand to her chest and then put her other hand on top of the first, astonished at the luxury of that other powerful sense: touch.

Had she known that she'd be this terrified? What was making her so scared? Knowing that they'd all be dropped out in the woods, forced to find their way to their campsite without GPS, in darkness? Or was it—and of course it more likely was—the fact that they were heading to the place where she'd last seen her father alive, a place that had so many positive memories of being with him, but also that would remind her, in so many little ways, of his death? It had been her choice to join the Scouts in Ede, so her dropping would be in the Hoge Veluwe Park. All the other options in the country had seemed too small and too tame—the Veluwe was a real national park where it would actually feel like going on safari, a place where you could actually get lost.

Her mom had asked her about a million times if this was really a good idea, but Karin had just insisted. She knew it so well, she had told her mom, and she needed to feel comfortable there, of all places, the place her father had treated like their own backyard. After a while, she'd heard her mom boasting to people that Karin was really "resilient"—that was the word parents used when they wanted to compliment you for not falling to pieces after your father died. Closer to the truth? She needed to prove to herself that she wasn't afraid. She could, she would, get over it.

But secretly, and now without her trusty vision and surrounded by basically strangers, she was afraid that maybe she couldn't, maybe she wouldn't. Maybe going out to that place, unaccompanied by adults, at night, was the worst possible idea she'd ever come up with. Her heart beat even faster when she thought these thoughts. Her head began to spin. She took a deep, deep breath in, trying to get her head back. *Yeah,* she thought, *what a really stupid idea.*

Ugh, why did her mom let her be so dumb? She was only twelve. She didn't know how to make decisions for herself. Okay, her head could stop spinning now. Time to focus on something else. Back to the task at hand: what could her senses tell her, without sight?

There were three of them in the back seat and one in the front passenger seat, of that much she was sure. She felt a leg beside her leg that was thin and soft, not muscular like a boy's. She got a whiff of perfume, the smell of rose water and cotton candy. That was a scent that came in a bottle in the shape of a ballerina or a swan. Karin really didn't like the smell of rose water. It was supposed to be a nice smell, she knew, but it reminded her of old ladies and bathrooms. But she definitely knew who that perfume belonged to, because she'd smelled it all summer: Margot.

Dirk, the only boy in their group, would then be on

the other side of Margot, by the right back door. He was maybe even trying to cop a feel of Margot while they both sat there in the made-up dark. She tried to hear if anything was happening between them, but there was no tittering or giggling, and it made her feel a little icky about herself to even be wondering about the two of them. She tried to brush the images of them out of her mind. If Dirk wasn't next to Margot, then he was in the front passenger seat. But she had a feeling it was Lotte up there. No idea why.

Before they got the blindfolds, they had been forced to hand over their smartphones. One of the leaders held out this black velvet bag and they had to drop them in there, like they were robbery victims handing off their diamonds to the thieves. Then the adults had gone through their backpacks to make sure they weren't carrying anything forbidden—an extra phone or a GPS or an electronic compass, or what, even?—and to make sure that none of them was smuggling beer or weed or any other contraband out into the woods. Some Scouts had been caught doing that before, and they'd been sent home immediately and the whole dropping cancelled. Karin hoped that none of the kids in her group would be that stupid, but she didn't know any of them all that well. So, yeah, they'd basically been fleeced of all their valuables by a bunch of adults, including her mother, and that felt weird.

Her own zebra-pattern backpack, which she'd packed with an extra set of dry clothes, her mess kit, her key chain with her mini flashlight, her compass, her water bottle, a yellow emergency rain poncho, a tinder kit, a pocket knife, some coins, dry noodles and oats (in case of emergency), and lots of "healthy" candy bars made of dates or tempeh or whatever, was then put in the trunk of the car.

Then they had made them all put on fluorescent-orange vests over their camel-colored Scout shirts and their fall jackets. This was a precaution so they wouldn't get hit by cars while they were stumbling around aimlessly, blind-folded. Some other kid had been hit by a car before the dropping had even started in exactly that scenario, a while ago, and everyone had been talking about that at the Scout Clubhouse.

Her mom, nodding, had said that she'd read that in the newspaper too. Her mom always knew the disaster stories in any potential scenario—she had to give her that. A few weeks ago Karin's mom had read aloud to her a story in the paper about how a kid had gotten shot in the forest by some hunters who saw something moving in the bushes and thought this twelve-year-old kid was an elk.

And all summer long her mom had been updating Karin on the progress of this lone wolf that had somehow made his way from Germany and ended up in the Veluwe forest. He had somehow met a mate there—even though there weren't supposed to be any wolves in the Netherlands anymore—and they had mated and now there were pups. So she had that to look out for. There were plenty of things to freak out about if you wanted to freak out about stuff, according to her mom.

Karin had a quick thought about the wolf, wondering about those pups, and her hands instinctively moved to find her phone so she could Google their latest movements. Oh, right. She didn't have that anymore. No way to Snapchat with her friends, to make funny faces and share selfies, no TikTok for watching videos of random people doing random dances. Not even color-by-number Sandbox. Of course calling her mother would not be allowed. It was strictly verboten under dropping rules. Which was kind of dumb. Because, yeah, what if?

No phone was almost like being naked. Her thumbs kind of throbbed with pointlessness. She imagined this must be like what Buddhist monks do. Nothing at all, just sitting there, *Ommmmm*, letting their minds drift from one random thing to another. It must be a lot harder than she knew to be a monk, though, like real mental torture. How long was this ride going to be anyway? And why wasn't the car even moving yet?

As if answering her thought, the driver-side door opened, someone climbed in, and the car tilted almost imperceptibly. There was a moment while the driver adjusted his seat and probably checked the rearview mirror. It had to be a he—maybe one of the dads, she thought—because his movements were abrupt and masculine in some undefinable way, definitely not like a mom's movements. It could be the man who had put on her seat belt, which might be worrying.

"Okay, kids, we're about to set off," he said. "It'll be thirty to forty minutes before we get to the drop point." He had a dry, deep voice, speaking louder than he needed to, as if wearing blindfolds made them deaf as well as blind, she thought. It definitely wasn't the voice of Karl, who had been their leader all summer and who was supposed to be the Scout guide on this dropping. Was he one of the parent volunteers? "I'm Rutger and I'll be driving you. Unfortunately, two Scout leaders from another group got sick and so some of the supervisors have been switched around, but we'll be fine. Just settle in and try to see if you can figure out where we're going. But don't take off the masks, and obviously no talking."

Karin tried to imagine what Rutger looked like, and the

first picture that came into her head was Rutger Hauer in *Blade Runner,* that completely freaky movie Frank had made her watch a part of that one time. That white-blond villain with the terrifying blue eyes, shirtless, creepily muscular. Yeah, basically if that guy was driving them, they were all doomed.

"Give me a second to set the car's GPS," he said. "I'm going to put in my earbuds so I can listen to the driving directions and you won't hear them. Just so you know."

He turned on the engine, put the car in gear, and started off. But he didn't get very far before it slowed. She felt it turn to the right and then suddenly jerk into reverse, heard the wheels crunching along gravel, backward. With her eyes covered, this felt more violent than it would if she had been able to see, she told herself. Within a moment, she heard the clutch move and the car jolt forward again.

She could hear the quiet ticking of the turn signal, and then the car swung to the left. They went a little distance before Rutger stopped and shifted into reverse. They rolled backward slowly, then jolted forward again. Was he lost or was he just a terrible driver? Karin knew that sometimes the leaders did this—made fake turns to disorient the kids so they wouldn't know exactly where they were headed.

What the heck? She literally had no idea how to have a sense of direction when she was blindfolded anyway. She turned her face to the window and inclined her temple toward it, feeling the draft coming through the open slit at the top of the glass, which hissed quietly, like a garden snake. *Sssssssssh.*

Was it unusual that neither of the Scout leaders they'd trained with over the summer, Karl and Ilvy, was coming with them? Her stepdad and the other guide, whoever that was going to be, were supposed to follow in another car, filled with all the camping gear and cooking supplies for the overnight. She listened for the sound of that second car behind them but didn't hear it. She had the instinct to turn around and look but realized that with the blindfold on it would be useless.

When Karin's forehead touched the cold glass of the car window, her thoughts began to drift in a new direction. She thought of how she'd woken up that morning, at home in her bed, in the house she now shared with her mom and her stepdad, Martijn, and her two stepbrothers, who were only there sometimes.

The feeling she'd had that morning came back to her, lying there in bed and listening to the sounds downstairs of them fighting. They fought a lot these days—over what, Karin had no idea. Then she remembered what had finally roused her from her bed: the sound of something crashing in the kitchen downstairs. The sound of her stepfather cursing. And that strange sound after that—a very loud thud— that somehow had rippled through her entire body and made it convulse. That thud was no good, and then that eerie silence.

CHAPTER 2

SEE YOU AGAIN TOMORROW

Grace and Martijn stood arm in arm in front of the Scout Clubhouse, waving the kids off, even though that made no real sense. None of them could see anything. As soon as the car was out of sight, they let go and looked at one another, sizing each other up as one might a sparring partner. Then Grace silently picked up the rest of Karin's equipment, sleeping bag, pillow, and rain tarp, and placed it in the back of the second car, an old Volkswagen.

Martijn would soon get into that car with Riekje, the sporty blond Scout leader, all of nineteen, who would be driving both of them to the camp, while Grace headed back to their house to have a much-needed night to herself. Glancing at the young woman, she felt only the quickest stab of jealous concern but almost immediately decided that if Martijn was into that whole scene, so be it. What she needed was a long bath and some time to catch up on the phone with her friends.

Grace gave the girl a wan smile, which was returned with an energetic leap in her direction and the sudden pumping of her hand.

"She's going to love it," Riekje said, perhaps misreading

Grace's weak smile as attachment anxiety. "The ones who are especially nervous on the way out always end up having the most fun. I promise you that," she quickly added.

Grace considered this a moment, wondering if Karin had appeared especially nervous at the send-off. If she had, had Grace failed to notice? Had she let her daughter go off on this adventure, what was supposed to be a kind of coming-of-age ritual, without her whole and undivided attention? After all, this was a particularly strange undertaking for Karin—spending the night in a forest that had, for all intents and purposes, belonged to her father.

She glanced over at Martijn to see if he had somehow picked up on Karin's emotional frequencies, but she doubted it. He was a good-enough stepdad but not really empathic in those kinds of ways. Still, she was pleased he had volunteered to go along on the trip as a parental supervisor. It wasn't his kid who was heading off into the forest, and his own children had done their droppings elsewhere. But it showed initiative that he'd taken the time to go along. She read it as an attempt to show that he cared about bonding with Karin. She liked that. Maybe, eventually, their families *would* blend.

"Thanks for your concern, but I don't have any doubt she'll be fine," Grace said to the Scout leader, and then wondered if she had sounded overly officious. But she couldn't tell her that she doubted Karin had even an ounce of nervousness. "I mean, I'm sure you're right," she added. "She'll love it."

Would she love it? Karin wasn't exactly a novice camper, since she'd had a lot of outdoor adventures with her father. The idea of the dropping was that she'd be out there with her peers, kids as uncertain and wobbly about the world and themselves as she was, and they'd have to rely on one another to find their way to the finish. Grace liked that aspect of this Dutch rite of passage; it was so unlike the American culture in which she'd grown up. The Americans talked a lot about self-reliance, but the Dutch put it into practice at an early age, by basically leaving their children alone and letting them figure things out.

Of course, the parents and the Scouts would never be far away. They would be there at the front end and at the back end. And if something went awry, they'd never be out of shouting distance.

The Scout Clubhouse was just outside Ede proper, in a low-lying white brick building built a half-century ago that looked like a vintage schoolhouse. It was surrounded by tall, thin birches, resembling high fence posts, that made it all seem very orderly. There was some playground equipment and a small pebbly beach that bordered a sizable lake, now deserted because the season was over.

Karin had lurched out of their car as soon as they pulled into the parking lot, running over to the other kids, her fellow Scouts, obviously pleased to escape the vehicle, where there had been a low hum of tension between Grace and Martijn throughout the ride down. They'd had a fight earlier that day. Grace, watching her go, had felt the guilt of not resolving the fight before getting into the car, and making her daughter stew in it. She and Martijn still had to learn how to let go and move on, not to carry around an argument after it was basically over. This was part of the challenge of trying to build a new marriage, to blend two wholly different families, while she also felt the tug of losing her daughter to the world.

That loss was happening now—not little by little, as it

had when she was a small child waddling off with uncertain giggles into the freedom of the untethered world, but in leaps and bounds as Karin found greater satisfaction in places outside the home than she did in the loving arms of her mother. Grace had tried to prepare herself mentally for this transition, since like all parents she knew it was the way with adolescents, but somehow all that internalized mental coaching didn't make it hurt any less. Could it be that her stress about that loss was actually making her testy with Martijn? Was that it? And nothing to do with him at all?

Karin's group was not the only group at the Scout Clubhouse. There were a few other droppings scheduled to begin this evening, in different parks in the region. None of the kids were supposed to know where they were headed—they had all been told it could be in one of the three nature reserves, the Hoge Veluwe National Park or the adjacent Veluwezoom National Park or the Utrechtse Heuvelrug, to the west of Ede. But Karin had specifically requested the Hoge Veluwe, because of her history with her father there, much to Grace's chagrin. What made a twelve-year-old kid think they had to go off and face their personal demons in the dark like that? Grace would never really know. But she did respect it, and was just a little bit proud of Karin.

Martijn ambled up to her and put a hand on her shoulder, startling her out of her thoughts. She turned to him and looked at his dour face, his unsmiling look, and his still so beautiful pale green eyes. The expression they held was not entirely devoid of love, but one might have to get out a miner's pickaxe and headlamp to find it. She noticed now how deep the wrinkles near his temples had become, how the grooves of his crow's feet appeared like rivulets

14

descending from the furrows of his brow. Had she done this to him? Made his eyes this sad and his skin so ashen?

"Grace, my Grace," was all he said in the low, bass voice he used when he wanted to sound like a soulful radio announcer. It felt good to hear some sweetness and levity in his tone again, to be reminded of his softer side. In the ensuing pause, as he looked at her more seriously, she heard the rest of what he meant to say: *We need to stop fighting, even if it means we need to quit one another. We can't keep doing this to each other.*

She nodded; he was right. Why couldn't they just come together and sort things out? They were hurting each other too much. It wasn't working.

"Are you ready?" she asked him. "Do you feel prepared for this adventure?"

It was meant to be a white flag. Surrender.

"They gave me the necessary information, I think," he said, dropping his eyes to the brown earth. "I'm just supposed to follow, and keep a distance so they don't know I'm behind them. If anything goes wrong, I'll catch them up and help out. Simple as that."

"And not sneak up on them like a bear? Not pretend to be a howling wolf in the distance?"

He smiled a half smile. "No Wolfman Jack."

And now, more seriously, she added, "You'll let me know if anything goes wrong? Or even just if Karin starts to feel strange?"

"I'm not supposed to get that close to them," he said. But added, "Of course."

"What time do you think you'll be back here tomorrow?"

"I suspect around this time. We're supposed to explore the park with the kids tomorrow, and there are some activities planned for the early afternoon, like a scavenger hunt. I'll call you when we're leaving base camp."

A fantasy flashed before Grace's eyes, a daydream or a vision, of using the time not to drive home, take a bath, and make longed-for phone calls but to make a grander escape, taking the car south and out of the Netherlands and just coasting farther on, through Europe, maybe till she hit Italy. She imagined Cinque Terre, that beautiful cluster of towns on the rugged Italian coast she'd visited once as a girl. But the daydream was as fleeting as a hummingbird, and was stopped in its tracks by the idea of Karin being left behind with Martijn and his sons. Whatever escape she made would always be with Karin.

"I'll plan to start driving down around two just to be on the safe side," Grace said.

She thought about how not twenty minutes ago she had stood with her daughter and watched as Karin had turned the blindfold over in her hands before putting it on, as a single tear rolled down her own cheek—unseen, she'd hoped.

"Mom, please?" Karin had whispered, irritated. "You don't have to be so American about it. I'll be back in, literally, twenty-four hours. You'll thank me for this. I mean, think about the time alone, with the house totally to yourself. When do you ever have that?"

The words had been so mature, coming from Karin, that she'd had to laugh, squeezing her daughter tightly to her. Only making matters worse.

Of course she realized it was a bit stupid. Karin had already been away longer on sleepovers at friends' houses. But Grace was vulnerable right now, in ways she couldn't articulate. She needed her daughter to be okay because her own personal life felt like a cabin made of popsicle sticks that could topple any moment.

"It's just…it's just that you're getting so big," Grace had told Karin, making a cliché out of the moment. "You're growing up so fast."

All Karin said was "Seriously, Mom" and rolled her eyes. "I won't be any older tomorrow."

Grace had given her daughter a tender smile. "You'll be a day older." Then she'd kissed her once more on the head and let her go. Karin had turned and joined the group, where she'd been told to put on her mask. She had probably been relieved to finally escape Grace's maternal gaze.

So the groups had assembled, the parents had completed their tasks, and the kids had been guided into their cars and driven away. It was true that this dropping felt far more poignant than she had expected it to, for so many complicated reasons. She'd need a month of therapy to fully unwind all the threads. She had been relieved, at last, to hear the sound of the car with the kids in it pull out; she could let go of holding her breath.

CHAPTER 3

DROP POINT

Karin heard the car slowing down, felt it turn off the road to the right, heard the tires come off the slick asphalt and crunch down onto an unpaved road. She could feel the automobile slip down into some kind of softer earth and then a loud rumble and vibration underneath the car. She knew that sound: they were passing over one of those metal grates that prevented deer from crossing into the Veluwe parking lot.

They had to be near the drop point, Karin was sure now. She felt excited and leaned forward in her seat, and then realized as a kind of weight fell over her that she was tired already. It was probably only like 5:15 now, the time when, at home, she'd be on her bed upstairs with her computer in her lap, trying to finish up her homework before dinner. She wasn't like her friends at school who loved to stay up late doing their homework together, but really just gossiping on Snapchat. Karin really liked to go to bed early. In fact, she'd put on her supersoft teddy-bear PJs right after helping her mom load the dishwasher. She didn't always fall asleep right away; usually, she stayed up reading magazines or books.

No one would see her in teddy-bear PJs here, no way.

She had brought only sweats and a T-shirt to sleep in. She wanted to show the kids that she was a little bit like her father, the famous war adventurer. But first she would have to muster the energy to get out of this car.

Dirk started singing, *"We zijn er bijna! We zijn er bijna!"* in Dutch, a song little kids sang when arriving somewhere (*"We're almost there!"*), and she could hear Lotte, in the front seat, laugh at this bit of self-mockery. Margot shushed Dirk, and Karin felt a movement of bodies that might have been Margot elbowing Dirk in the ribs, while Rutger took a hard tone. "As you know, no talking until we arrive at the drop point," he said. Everyone was quiet again after that.

They rode in silence again for another fifteen minutes or so—Karin tried to time it in her head, to be able to calculate about how far they would be from the main road if they had to find it later. Maybe it was more like ten, or it could have been twenty, but honestly it was so hard to tell how long things took when you couldn't just check your phone.

The car pulled up onto what seemed like a hill and stopped. "All right," said Rutger. "You all stay put and I'll come around and open the doors for you." Like they were invalids all of a sudden. Was there really going to be sideswipe danger, as they'd been warned? Karin couldn't hear any cars anywhere nearby. Actually, she heard only crickets. As if reading her thoughts, Rutger said, "It's just that I don't want you to fall because you can't see where you're going."

So he grabbed them one by one, with his rough hands and hot breath, which now smelled like he'd accented it with mints, and seemed to be lining them up in a row on the dirt. Karin felt like a prisoner in a World War II movie, getting readied for the firing squad. She let a shiver of that feeling crawl up her spine before deciding that it was maybe better not to spook herself more with morbid fantasies. There were enough ghosts in this forest to do that already.

At long last, Rutger told them they could take off the blindfolds. Karin reflexively drew her hand up to cover her eyes, blinking several times to get used to seeing again. It was weird that her eyes had to adjust to the light after such a short time blindfolded, and especially because it was not very bright out anymore. The sun was already showing signs of setting. She welcomed back her primary sense and took in the view.

In front of them was a sandy park road for cars, which wound down to the right toward a grove of trees and then ended where the forest turned into heath. To the left, way down that way, the road met the paved national park road. Without turning, she knew that behind her lay a bike path that abutted a parallel hiking trail.

"We're near the south gate," she announced, mostly to herself. "And right there is Stag's Wood." She pointed at a wooden tower about the size of a treehouse, where she'd spent hours with her father waiting for red deer to emerge.

"You've got to be kidding me," said Dirk, giving her a once-over. "You already know where we are?"

Margot piped up, "Wow, that's impressive, nature lover."

Smiling inwardly so as not to gloat, Karin wondered if Margot's comment was for real or kind of a sarcastic jab. *Nature lover?* She turned away from the two of them, took a deep breath in, and drank down the fresh, clean air of the forest. The scent of pine needles filled her nose. It was okay. This was where she'd been so many times with her dad. It couldn't be scary; and the other kids couldn't unsettle her. She would be okay here.

Rutger stood in front of the car they'd arrived in—a silver minivan, it turned out—like he was waiting for them to do something. He didn't look anything like the guy from that freaky movie. He was a little pudgy, with a rust-colored beard and mustache, and a face that was both long and overly wide. What was left of the hair on top of his head he had brushed over to make it look thicker, but when the wind picked up—as it did at just that moment—there was almost nothing there, just fluffy, ruddy strands flying everywhere.

"Karl and Ilvy were both supposed to be your guides today, but unfortunately Ilvy wasn't feeling very well and Karl took over Group 3, so I took Ilvy's place," Rutger started to explain. "Martijn, Karin's father, will be coming along soon with Riekje, one of the Scout leaders from Group 3. They should be arriving any minute."

"Stepfather," Karin said, quick as a stab.

"Uh," Rutger said, slow to the uptake.

"Martijn is not my father," Karin said. "He's married to my mother, but my dad was someone else. He died."

"Oh," said Rutger. "Yes, I see. I'm sorry."

Karin shrugged, letting them all know it didn't matter to her anymore.

None of the kids said anything, but Lotte glanced over at her to read her face. Karin tried to keep her expression totally neutral and wondered who here knew her family story. Her father's death had been in the national news, after all, but who knew if they watched the news, or if they had taken the time to put the puzzle pieces together. Or if they cared anyway.

Rutger then looked away from her and explained what would happen next, even though they'd heard it a million times already. The Scouts would have to find their way to the campsite together, using only their compasses and nature itself. There would be hot chocolate and sausages waiting for them when they got there.

It didn't matter how long it took them, and they shouldn't feel rushed, but they were expected to arrive sometime before 8 p.m., and ideally around 7 p.m., so they could eat their hot dogs and enjoy the campfire under the night sky before tucking in for the night. If they got lost, they should just keep going, keep working together until they could find their way. The Scout leaders wouldn't set out to find them unless they hadn't arrived by morning. They laughed at that—it wouldn't take them *all night, obviously.*

The main thing was that they needed to stay together and work as a group, be patient with one another; help each other out, stay on track, and avoid wild animals. The kids all nodded in unison: *Right, right. Sure, sure.*

After that, they took their backpacks out of the trunk and double-checked their supplies. They drank water and refilled their bottles with the big jug Rutger had in the back of his minivan. Then they just stood around, waiting for a while at the clearing in the woods, awkwardly, not saying much, for the second car to arrive. Looking out across the hilly landscape, Karin saw lots of patches of purple heath and little tufts of grass, like beards of old men, everywhere.

After a little while, Rutger walked away from the group and fished his cell phone out of his bag—he had it only for emergency purposes, he said—and tried calling Martijn and Riekje. "Strange," he said, coming back, his wisps of hair floating for a moment over his head. "No answer. But they'll probably be along shortly."

Dirk, impatient by now, said the group was losing time, and he wanted to get started. "They aren't supposed to go with us anyway," he said. "We can start." Lotte and Margot were opposed. They didn't really want to deviate from the plan. Karin was with Dirk. The point was to do it on their own, anyway, right? Rutger looked miffed. "Let's just wait a little longer," he said.

The kids stood around, kicking the dirt, which was dry like sand and burst into the air as dark puffs.

"Did anyone hear about the wolf?" Dirk asked.

"What wolf?" said Lotte.

"Oh, come on, don't try to scare us," said Margot with a flirty twitter. "There are no wolves here."

Dirk straightened up, excited to be urged on. "There are. Haven't you read? Wolves are back in the Netherlands after, like, more than a hundred years."

"A hundred forty years," Karin said, realizing too late that she was sounding really annoying. But it was true. "My mom is obsessed with the wolves," she added with a shrug. "I get a daily play-by-play."

The kids glanced at her warily, but Dirk seemed chuffed that his story was confirmed by the nature nerd. He nodded for her to continue, and she took the invitation.

"There used to be wolves here a long time ago, but then they, like, kind of wandered off to Germany." Karin knew the right word for this was "migrated" but was loath to use any even mildly scientific language among her peers. "And they've lived there for a long time, but then one of them just showed up here by himself last year. A male. And then later somehow there was a female, and early this summer they had pups."

"Awwww," Lotte said, as if Karin had been telling a love story.

"Wait, so now it's, like, a whole wolf family?" Margot said. "How many?"

"I don't know," Karin said, although she did know. "Maybe, like, six or seven?"

There were seven. Karin had seen photos of five wolf cubs born in June. Her father, if he were still alive, would have definitely come out here to take pictures of them. That had been his thing. And she would have come with him, definitely.

"So there's, like, a wolf *pack* out here?" Margot asked, her eyes bulging out, totally exaggerating. "In these woods?"

Could Margot and Lotte have missed the boat on this whole story? The story was, like, everywhere. Karin had spent the summer dodging the subject every time she mentioned her upcoming dropping to an adult. *"Ah, Roodkapje, Roodkapje, waar ga je heen?"* ("Red Riding Hood, Red Riding Hood, where are you going?") they'd start singing, the song from the Dutch Little Red Riding Hood movie everyone watched.

"See?" said Dirk, now very satisfied with himself even though he had said literally nothing.

"Yeah, but they wouldn't hurt people." Karin kind of wanted to take some wind out of his sails. "It's not like Little Red Riding Hood. Wolves eat sheep or deer. They would only attack you if you tried to hurt their babies."

"I don't know," Dirk said, darting her a look. "I see three pretty tasty *Roodkapjes* right here."

"O-M-G, you guys are not serious," said Margot. "We're

not going out there to be eaten by wolves! I'm about to turn back right now and go home."

Karin turned to Dirk. "You don't need to scare everyone. I read the family had probably moved on by now anyway. They have to get somewhere warm by winter." This was a lie, but no one was fact-checking.

Dirk just lifted his chest and leaned his head back and howled, "Aahwooooh! Aaahooowh!" at the top of his lungs. "Maybe he'll howl in response…"

All of them waited to hear if there was an echo to his howl. There was none.

"Literally?" said Margot, giving him an exasperated look. "I can't believe you are literally trying to get the wolves to speak to you."

Dirk looked at all three girls, with the range of expressions on their faces, and a wide grin grew on his face. "You guys are too easy," he said. "Are you also afraid of the Wolfman? Because that's who I turn into late at night, when the moon is full." He looked up toward the sky, but they couldn't see the moon because of the clouds, and if it was up there, it probably wasn't full. "I come out here to see my old friends Freddy Krueger and Ghostface too." With that, he reached out to grab Margot, and she jumped.

"Don't!" she said. "You're totally scaring me." But instead of acting scared and pulling away, she tucked herself under Dirk's arms and tried to wrap herself in them, like a blanket.

He welcomed the invitation and put his big, wrestling-team arms around her shoulders, then slid them down to her waist. "Don't worry, little Margot. I'll make sure no wolves eat you!" He was laughing, and Margot clearly enjoyed the embrace, but her face pretended to have a pouty expression.

Lotte, seeing the two of them flirting in this way, puffed out "Whatever" and marched off toward the car. Karin claimed to have forgotten something in her backpack, though no one was listening anyway, and scampered off too. She didn't even bother pantomiming that one. As soon as she walked over to Lotte, the two of them leaned against the minivan and watched as Dirk and Margot tussled playfully with each other.

Lotte said softly, "Once, my family went camping in the South of France in the summer and we heard wolves howling the whole night through. I was so happy that we had a cabin and not just a tent. And in the morning, when we woke up, everyone was talking about how the wolf had come to our camping area and made off with someone's pet rabbit. I don't even understand why someone would bring a pet rabbit camping with them. How stupid is that?"

"That does sound kinda stupid," agreed Karin.

Karin and Lotte continued to lean against the car in silence. Right now she could really use her cell phone. She could check Instagram or find out what was trending on YouTube or even look at a Google map. But no. They just had to stand there like idiots next to each other with nothing to say.

Their eyes wandered up toward the sky. It was really overcast but not entirely covered. Some clouds looked like hillsides and others like shorelines. There was a tiny bit of light cresting over one of the clouds, like it was hoping for an entrance.

Rutger, who had walked off a distance to talk on his phone, bounded back over to them, his hair flapping on his head like a toupee. "Great, they're on their way!" he said. "They said they'd be here in about ten minutes. I've got their blessing to let you go ahead. Otherwise it'll be too late when you get to the campsite."

Without a word, Dirk hefted his backpack over his shoulder and walked off down the bike path. The girls looked at one another quizzically and Lotte shouted after him, "Why are you going that way?"

Without turning around, he shouted, "I thought we decided this was the way to go."

"We didn't decide anything," said Lotte, but it was no use. Dirk was the only boy in the group and so he thought he would appoint himself the leader, and now the three of them either had to follow and catch up with him or else forfeit the only requirement of the dropping: to stay together as a group.

"Come on," Margot said to the other girls, a girlfriend wannabe. "That way is as good a way as any."

CHAPTER 4

REFLECTIONS ON THE LAKE

Grace looked up at Martijn, whose eyes were absently following Riekje's movements as she got the final gear for the trip into the old Volkswagen. The Scout leaders had had a debriefing with all the parents involved in all the droppings, and now the second car—and Martijn—were about to leave the Scout Clubhouse.

Why was it that whenever they were alone, without Karin or his kids, or some other kind of company, she felt a kind of generalized anxiety, with her heart racing?

"I'm really sorry about this morning," he said to Grace, leaning down to kiss her goodbye.

Her reaction, completely involuntary, was to flinch and pull away. As soon as she'd done it, she wished she could take it back. She knew he would pick up on this, and it wouldn't help. "I know," said Grace, putting a hand on his arm, trying to compensate. "I'm sorry too."

His face fell. "Oh, so it's like that?" he said. "Really?"

During the fight this morning things had become too heated. She'd told him that he didn't have to be so angry; he'd screamed that he wasn't angry. She'd thought to show him his face in the mirror, so red, eyes glaring. He would be able to see that he was, indeed, angry. But when she had pulled him toward the mirror, he'd pushed her. Shoved her, actually, right up against the kitchen cabinets. She was sure he hadn't tried to hurt her, but the handle of a cabinet door had sliced through her shirt.

She reached up and drew his face toward hers, trying to be tender. She felt Martijn's soft lips meet her own, and she stayed there for a moment, letting the sweetness of this connection linger, the tingle of lust they still had between them. "No, of course not, honey."

He pulled back gently and studied her eyes. Then he walked out of the cul-de-sac where the cars were parked and toward the Scout Clubhouse. She dutifully followed him, footsteps crunching in the pebbles of the path.

He turned back toward her, looking defeated. "It's a mess right now, but we can sort it out," he said. "You know I didn't mean all that this morning. I certainly regret what I did; I feel sick about it. I'm not like that. I never want to hurt you." He moved closer, putting his arm around her shoulder and drawing her face to his kiss. "I want it to be better with us."

The embrace, after so much tension, made her chest feel heavy, and she knew she might cry if she didn't hold it back. She swallowed and looked up at him.

"Look, I don't want to get into it again. Let's let it go for now," Grace said, trying to keep calm, her voice controlled. "All I want to say is that I think it would help if we got a little counseling together. It would probably only take a few sessions. What we have is so strong, Martijn. But sometimes it becomes too intense. It scares me. I feel...anxious."

She hoped that this show of her vulnerability would crack open a door to him. That he would tell her the last thing he wanted was for her to feel anxious around him. But he shook his head. "Grace, come on," he said. "It hasn't even been a year that we've been living together. If we need therapy now, what does that say about our future?"

"It doesn't matter what it says," she answered. "Nobody is counting. I mean, it says that we care about the relationship we have and we want to make sure we get off to a good start. To make sure that we set off on a good footing. That we embark with the wind in the right direction—"

"And other metaphors," he cut her off, but with a smile.

Martijn's attitude toward therapy actually infuriated her. Was it the same aversion men had to asking for directions? If you had to ask for help, it meant you were weak? Grace was the kind of person who loved consulting anyone who might know something better than she did. She had stacks of books on her bedside table on all kinds of improvement categories—*You as Your Best Self, How to Find Common Ground with Anyone, Loving Unconditionally, What Makes a Happy Stepmom?, Dealing with Anger in Your Relationship*. It was rather an embarrassment, actually, but on the other hand, why be ashamed? She was a woman who wanted to be the optimal version of herself. Martijn told her she was "too Oprah."

In any case, at this very moment, Grace desperately did not want to get into a marital dispute, if this could really be classified as such, right here at the Scout Clubhouse, just before her husband left to volunteer for her daughter's camping trip. Especially since he was putting himself out there to show how much he cared about Karin, it would be a disgrace.

"It's not that I don't believe in therapy; I'm sure it can be good for some people," he volunteered, without her having to say what she had been thinking. "It's just that I think we can do this on our own. You just have to understand that I'm a little bit damaged, and, well, my kids are a little bit damaged too. And sometimes we just need you to give us the benefit of the doubt."

This logic had its self-effacing element, Grace understood, but it also cut in the opposite direction. It blamed her, didn't it, for not being patient and forgiving and generous enough. Was that really how it was?

She could go to therapy alone, of course, if he refused to come. She had heard people say that as soon as one side disarms, the battle necessarily ends. But what if she laid down her own defenses and his agitation remained? She'd trusted Martijn with everything until now; she'd put so much into his hands, her very life, and Karin's life too.

"So you're saying I'm not patient enough?"

Martijn spoke more softly. "No, no, no. It's just—it's me. I'm just dealing with a lot right now. I've got a lot on my plate, as you like to say. I'm trying to deal with a few too many things at once."

"With what?" Grace genuinely wanted to understand. "With us? With work?"

He looked around, as if he was assessing how much to reveal in this public place.

"Please," she said. "Can't you just tell me if there is something outside of the marriage—outside of us—that is putting pressure on you? If I knew what it was, maybe we could address it together. Before you go, couldn't you just articulate, a little, what is making you feel so stressed?"

He nodded and motioned her toward the lake. They walked together, their bodies aligned and their hands adjacent, without touching. Grace felt that if he would just take

31

her hand, reassure her a little bit, she could make it through without worrying. But he didn't.

Once they'd gotten some distance from the others, she said, "Okay, are you ready to tell me what is going on?"

He shook his head, lowering it to gaze at the ground. He looked back up into her eyes, his own shiny with moisture, if not tears. "I know I can't live up to your standards, to what you really deserve, Grace, to what…"—he hesitated, and she knew what he was about to say—"to what he might have been able to give you." They both knew that Martijn was referring to Pieter, but he wouldn't say the name out loud. "I feel that I'm not the man I should be for you. And never will be. I'll never be enough. It frightens me."

Grace, for the briefest moment, felt pity for Martijn. He was being really vulnerable here. It was quite a thing for him to say, actually. And she wanted to give him the answer he was seeking—that of course he was enough, she loved him just as much as or more than she had loved Pieter, and he was what she wanted. But unfortunately he was right, on a fundamental level. Neither she nor Karin would ever be able to love him the way they had loved Pieter. Pieter had been her first, true love and Karin's biological father. What could she do about that? It was impossible for her to lie to him.

Martijn stood there, looking simultaneously plaintive and afflicted. Grace saw in the wrinkles of his face, his beautiful green eyes, the desperation in his expression, that he contained a deep well of resentment toward her and maybe even a measure of fear. This was the expression of a man who had married a woman who wouldn't completely adore him in the way he wished. And she knew in her own heart, no matter how hard she tried to wish it away, that he was right.

But then, mingled almost immediately with her empathy for Martijn, came another, and equally powerful, emotion, that of scorn. There was something of a manipulation behind this show of vulnerability. Wasn't it a little ridiculous of Martijn to be envious of her feelings for a man who was dead? For a man with whom she'd spent half her lifetime and a man she'd lost to violence? For Karin's actual father? This was an unreasonable expectation, was it not?

And after that, a third, stranger feeling: that all of this was an act. A kind of emotional tactic, to cast blame her way and to deflect from his own failures as a husband. After all, wasn't it he who had been avoiding contact with her, staying up late in his office, refusing to even eat dinner with the family or address the way the boys were basically bullying her daughter?

No. She brushed the thought away. He wasn't being manipulative. He was trying to be genuine, but he just wasn't very good at it. Grace loved Martijn—it had to be love, what she felt for him, didn't it?—not a passionate love but a quiet, contented, knowing kind of love that she hoped meant stability for her and for Karin. Couldn't that be enough?

That was what she had thought going into the marriage. After almost a year of sharing a home, trying to raise three kids together who belonged not to the two of them but to other parents from other histories, it was hard. That was all. It was fucking hard. And they didn't have that baseline of a history and foundation to fall back on. All they had was who they were, deeply flawed and hurting individuals with a bunch of bad habits that shone brightly under the floodlights of cohabitation.

Grace turned away and continued to walk, through the playground, down the pebble beach, and toward the lake, which was remarkably still on this autumnal evening. The surface of the water, so dark and free of ripples, created a perfect mirror of the other shore, a ring of small summer cottages with boating docks out back, now shuttered for the season. The mirror of the water also revealed to her a suddenly threatening sky, heavy with gray clouds.

She thought how forlorn this playground and beachfront was, remembering how just a few months ago this same lake had been full of laughing children, gliding off the metal slides propped on wooden docks farther out in the water. How the little kids, in their flower-patterned bathing suits with their candy-colored water toys, had splashed and paddled close to the shore. Summer had been here not so long ago. How quickly they'd reached a far more desolate season.

Martijn had followed her to the edge of the lake, and he was watching her from a few yards away. She could feel his gaze on her, waiting for her to say something else, to give him a sign. Was it neediness he was trying to convey?

She knew that this was the moment for her to reassure him that he was enough. That was the right move now, the only way forward. But the best she managed to offer was "Martijn, I hate that you feel you're not enough. I don't want you feeling that."

She could see from his expression, angry and defeated, that it wasn't what he wanted to hear.

"Are you sure that there isn't something going on with you?" she asked. "Something that doesn't have to do with me, or us? I don't know. I just have this feeling that something isn't right. You spend so much time in your office upstairs, and it seems like your energy is not really focused. Something is making you, well, edgy. Can you tell me what it is?"

Martijn took a few steps toward her and put his hands on

both her shoulders from behind. "You're so good at sensing things. It's true. There is something that's been bothering me—not about us, just work," he said. "It's not worth discussing because it's almost over. Let's just let it go for now. I'll tell you about it when we're back home."

So there was something. Something outside of the two of them. Maybe he was going through a moment and they would get past it.

"Okay," she said, turning to face him. "I'm so glad you can tell me at least that. Let's use this night apart to calm down, and we can talk about it all with more sensible heads tomorrow. Let's take this opportunity to think things over."

"Think things over?" he asked, as if she'd meant it as a kind of threat. "About our future?"

"Just a little breather, to figure out where we stand," she said. "You'll be out here under the night sky in the forest air—that will help. I'll go home, relax, unwind, maybe binge-watch some nonsense on TV. Let's just think about ourselves and what we can do better, and tomorrow maybe we'll have more energy, so we can think about ways that we can find our way back to each other."

She hoped this would have a calming effect, but right away she could tell she'd missed her mark. He gazed down at the empty beach for a while. And then he muttered, "Sometimes you talk to me just like I'm a child." He had said it mostly to himself, then he turned on his heels and marched away, in fact just like an angry child.

Grace was at least allowed to stand there looking out across the lake, watching the sky darken in the water's reflection.

CHAPTER 5

BREATHE

"Um, yoooooo!" Karin cried out, trying to get Dirk to stop marching on ahead of everyone. She was all the way in back, probably too far for him to hear her. They were walking in order of self-importance, thought Karin: Dirk, Margot, Lotte... She called, "We're supposed to look at the map together and check our compasses, remember?"

It was kind of a thing now, to try to stay with Dirk and Margot when they obviously wanted to be alone. A few months earlier Karin had noticed that Margot had a crush on Dirk. It seemed like it took a while before he responded to Margot, but then suddenly they had a little thing going. During Scout hours, in front of the adults, they hid it all pretty well, but anyone could tell if they saw the way they looked at each other when grown-ups were out of the room.

Karin had never had enough of a real conversation with Dirk to be able to find out how he'd ended up in the Scouts in the first place. His presence there, among the gentle and shy preteeners who marveled over a butterfly's wings or camouflaged insects, seemed completely random. Maybe his parents had enrolled him as some form of punishment?

Maybe to force him to be more down-to-earth? Dirk lived in Amsterdam and went to secondary school there—one of the private ones, she heard—and he was a wrestler, or had been. That made sense. Being a Scout didn't.

Since no one was answering, she tried again, only much louder: "*Haallooo?* We need to figure out where we are and where we're going."

This finally stopped Dirk in his tracks. If he'd stopped any more abruptly, he and Margot would've banged into each other, like an old slapstick act in one of those black-and-white TV shows her mother watched. "I thought you knew exactly where you were at all times," he said, not hiding his sarcasm.

Karin shrugged. "Well, even if I did, you're not exactly following me," she said. "But anyway, I don't want to be the leader. Dropping rules say we're supposed to find our way together."

"Dropping rules," he said with a laugh that sounded more like a grunt. "You're such a rule follower. I say it can't be that hard. There aren't so many trails."

Karin knew that was wrong. "There are, like, more than a hundred trails in this forest. Like, tons."

That seemed to convince Dirk, but he didn't backtrack, just waited for Karin to catch up to him and the other girls. The Scout leaders had given them one map, but they didn't know who had it. They all had to check their backpacks, and it turned out to be in Lotte's. "I've got it!" she cried out, like she'd won the lottery or something. She unfolded it carefully, gift wrapping she planned to reuse. It was too big to hold open by herself, so Margot held one side and Lotte held the other. Karin and Dirk hovered over it, but Karin was stuck looking at it upside down.

"Where did you say we drove in?" Dirk asked Karin. "Stud something?"

Karin paused for a weighty second before she said, "Stag's Wood. Seems like we must have driven in through the Schaarsbergen entrance," Karin said. She knew from coming here with her father that there were three car entrances to the park and two places where you could pick up white bikes to cycle around. The south entrance was where you went if you wanted more nature, the west entrance if you wanted to go to the museum, and the north one took you to this kind of weird castle-like house where the people who once owned the whole forest used to live, back in the 1920s or something.

"That would be here," said Lotte, stabbing her index finger onto the *P* in the little box that indicated parking. "But we're not there anymore. I don't know if we went north or west or what."

Karin turned around and saw the sun on the horizon, orange and blazing, and backed by a ribbon of purplish blue. "The sun rises in the east and sets in the west," she said, trying really hard not to sound pedantic. When no one said anything, she added, "So that's west," pointing.

"Uh, duh," Dirk said.

Karin, embarrassed, looked at the others to see if they agreed. Margot wasn't exactly paying attention. She seemed to be using the moment of gathering around the map to press her boobs against Dirk's arm and looked like she was daydreaming about something completely unrelated.

"I agree with Karin," she put in chirpily. "She's the one who knows what we're doing. Let's just follow her."

Dirk looked over his shoulder at Margot. "I'm not following her," he said.

Margot took an uneasy step back.

"Um, should we use our compasses?" Lotte suggested.

"Good idea," agreed Karin, pointing to Lotte.

They all found their backpacks again, Dirk and Margot groaning, and fished around for their old-fashioned metal disks with spinning metal arrows inside. Using the magnetic force of the world, they tried to orient themselves. For Karin, it just confirmed that west was in the location of the setting sun, as it should be, but at least it was quiet for a little while.

Lotte used due north to find where they might be on the map. "Could we be here?" she said, mostly to Karin.

"I'm kind of in a bad position to see it," admitted Karin. "Can I come around over there?"

"Oh, I thought for sure you could read it upside down and backward," said Dirk.

"And standing on your head," said Margot, trying to win back some of Dirk's favor.

They jostled and moved, with Lotte still holding one side of the map and Margot holding the other, and somehow in the commotion to let Karin take a look, the map ripped in two. Margot fell over, kind of overdramatically, with her half, and Dirk swooped down and grabbed it, putting a hand out to lift Margot. "Hey, cool," he said. "Now we have two maps!"

Without any warning, Dirk took off in a sprint, and Margot followed. "I guess you'll have to catch us if you want the other half!" Dirk yelled back to Karin and Lotte, who stood glaring from a distance. He panted up a big grassy hill and disappeared over the other side.

The two girls stood looking at each other. "What the...?" Karin said.

"He's such a . . ." Lotte said quietly, not finishing with whatever curse word she would never allow herself to say. Then she let out a heavy sigh. "I guess we'd better chase them, then."

"Really?" said Karin, feeling defeated already. She could not believe this. It would be a really, really long night if they kept up this way. But then, after Lotte took off in a sprint, she ran.

The two of them bounded over a sandy hill covered with tall grasses, which scraped against their ankles. Karin figured they'd see Dirk and Margot as soon as they rounded a bend in the path, but when they got there, there was no sign of either of them. Lotte was panting pretty hard just from that sprint—she was kind of overweight and didn't do any sports—but they nodded at each other and kept running. Dirk and Margot had to be here somewhere. Karin thought maybe they'd somehow found a hiding place in the grass, but it was hard to imagine where.

After a while, they came to a large downed tree that was so dried out that it was the color of silver and looked like a kind of driftwood statue. They slowed, then stopped for a minute to catch their breath. "Huh," said Lotte. "This is so weird."

Just then, Dirk came screaming out of the bushes, lunging at their feet and toppling Lotte. Margot stepped out a couple of seconds later and stood pointing and laughing. "Ha, he got you! He really got you!"

Karin wanted to laugh so that she wouldn't seem totally stiff, but she couldn't make herself do it. That was just mean to Lotte, and mean wasn't her kind of funny.

It took them all a minute to realize that Lotte, who was lying flat on her back on the sand, also wasn't laughing, and wasn't getting up. In fact, she seemed like she was having trouble breathing. She took tiny sips of air into her lungs, like she was winding up to cry. Her eyes, now directed at Karin, were wide and teary, but she wasn't crying, she was stuck on the ground, kind of . . . choking.

"Aw, don't be like that," Dirk said, walking off, like he'd had nothing to do with it. "I didn't hit you that hard. You're exaggerating."

"What's happening?" said Margot. "Is she kidding?"

Karin knelt down over Lotte as the girl's eyes, behind her glasses, started to look even more frantic. Karin put a hand on Lotte's shoulder and put her face close to Lotte's mouth to listen to her breathe.

"You knocked the wind out of her," Karin said. "She can't breathe."

"Come on!" said Dirk, like Karin was making it up just to bother him. "I was playing around."

Karin reserved the look of disdain she really wanted to shoot at him and instead sat down on the sand next to Lotte. "You're okay," she said gently, "but you've got to get breathing again. Here, let me help you sit up." She dug a hand under Lotte's back and pulled her up into a seated position, while Margot just gawped and Dirk literally walked off into the dunes, cursing. "You've got to try to take a few deeper breaths, maybe holding the air deep in your lungs." Karin had learned all this playing hockey. She'd been on a team for a few years when she was younger, until her father died. She'd seen a bunch of girls lose their breath this way, and it had happened to her once too, so she knew how scary it could feel, and she was afraid for Lotte.

Lotte tried heaving her chest up, but that didn't work. "Slower," said Karin, and Lotte gazed at her like she was a

41

life raft. She breathed slower, taking a sip of air this time. Then another. "Good," said Karin. "Slow like that." Little by little, Lotte got back to breathing normally. She was pretty upset, though. When she finally was ready to stand up, Karin gave her a hand and Margot came rushing over to try to help too, but it was too late. "Don't come near me," said Lotte, kind of croaking it out. "Your stupid boyfriend is a dick." There, thought Karin, she'd said it.

Margot stepped backward, as if pushed. "Um, he's not my *boyfriend*. And anyway, it's not his fault you fell down."

"What??" said Lotte, looking to Karin for confirmation.

Margot was a gymnast in school. Karin knew she did competitions and everything. During Scouts she was always doing cartwheels and handstands and sometimes even splits, out of nowhere. She showed off her perfect stomach with crop tops and low-rider jeans. They always had way too many rips, all the way from the top to the knees—the kind of pants Karin's mom would never let her wear. If Karin was going to take bets, she was sure Margot could easily take Lotte, if it came to a girl fight. She really didn't want that to happen.

"You're the dick," Margot said, but only kind of half committed to saying it.

Lotte blinked in a really obvious way and cocked her head to one side. "Um, not possible?" She pressed her glasses, which had been all tilted, back onto her nose.

"I don't even believe you couldn't breathe," Margot added for no reason. "You were totally faking it."

Lotte kind of coughed, and not even on purpose, just because she was still trying to get her breathing back on track. It was so obvious she wasn't faking, thought Karin, it didn't even make sense for Margot to be this mean.

"Uh, yeah…" said Lotte, turning her back on Margot. Karin was proud of her for doing that.

It was turning into two against two, which really wasn't cool, Karin knew. It would take forever to get to the campsite if they were constantly fighting like this. Karin didn't want to act like she was the schoolteacher in the group; she just wanted everyone to get back to the *point*. The trail, the trip, the campsite.

The three girls stood there for a minute and it was pretty tense. Karin had a lot she wanted to say, but she held it in. They all looked at one another, and for a split second Karin thought they were all going to start laughing.

Then there was this crazy howling noise coming from up the hill, and they all looked up to see Dirk kind of leaping into the air above them. He had a huge silver branch of that downed tree, which he was wielding above his head with both hands.

"I'm a samurai!" he cried, making a whooping noise as he swung the branch around in the sky. "Who dares challenge me?"

CHAPTER 6

FROM THERE TO HERE

Grace drove herself home, wishing she'd remembered to bring her earbuds with her so she could call her friends immediately and catch up. As a passenger with Martijn at the wheel on the drive down, she had determined that she would use this weekend to discover her inner Zen, take a bath and unwind with a good book. But now that everyone was gone, and she was on her own for the first time in actual months, she felt a kind of rare exhilaration. She could do anything, go anywhere, make all her own choices. No one to answer to for a full twenty-four hours.

It had been so long since she'd seen Krista, Nicolien, or Thomas, or even any of the mothers from school, for that matter. Before they'd married, this circle of friends had been such close confidants, but lately Grace had felt increasingly closed off from them. Maybe it was her embarrassment about how badly things were going with Martijn. All the rest of them were so happily settled. And they'd been so happy for her, especially after losing Pieter, that she'd found this new situation. Or maybe she'd reduced her contact with them out of a sense that Martijn disapproved of her turning elsewhere for comfort, relying on anyone other than him.

She had this sneaking suspicion that whatever was wrong with them wasn't the normal kind of wrong. It probably couldn't be fixed with a little extra sugar or salt or milk. She feared it was somehow more fundamentally flawed, like an instant yeast that simply doesn't rise. What was it? Was it really his work that was making him so distracted?

In the beginning, Grace had jumped into the relationship with both feet; she had ached so badly to have a new partner after losing Pieter that it was possible she had not been sufficiently circumspect. Two years of stellar sex with this absurdly handsome man who was a good earner and a responsible father had seemed like enough. *Let's take this check to the bank and cash it* was her attitude. Why muddle around?

But what did she know about him, really, before they tied the knot? She knew his body and his emotional seasons, his daily ablutions and how he took his coffee (with a surprising amount of milk for a European, she felt). She understood his basic morality, if you could call his modern belief system such. She never had asked him much about his work—accounting wasn't exactly a topic that invited inquiry, and he was never particularly forthcoming about the daily dramas of his job, if there were any. But what did he do up there, in his office?

She'd met Martijn's estranged father and his wife, but only about a week before the wedding, because they lived "far away" by Dutch standards, up in the Frisian Islands, about two and a half hours by car. The man seemed polite, if extremely reserved, and the wife appeared to have taken over all the social tasks for the both of them, responding rather loudly to any question directed at him, in a thick Frisian accent that Grace found incomprehensible.

Martijn didn't have siblings; his mother had died when he was just five, and he'd grown up with his dad and a Jack Russell terrier named Hanro. He barely spoke about his early years, but Grace got the feeling they were lonely and drearily metaphysical, like a George Eliot novel, a boy wandering around in the wet northern heath.

Grace could still remember the time she'd met Martijn's first wife, Lila, introduced in the narrow hallway of her Amsterdam apartment, on the top floor of a titled canal house, converted from an attic. The woman had given her a dour look that spoke volumes of a Dostoevskian length. Had Grace stopped to try to decipher the meaning behind her eyes she might have prepared herself for this marriage differently—how, she couldn't really imagine— but she hadn't taken the time to translate even one sentence of that manuscript. Exes always had grievances, though. Grace, for her part, had been light and easy, carried on the butterfly wings of lust. Sure of everything.

No more. Now she was decidedly unsure.

When she finally reached their house—she couldn't even remember any part of the scenery during the forty-five-minute drive, so deep in her head had she been—she walked up the front stairs, unlocked the front door, went inside, shut the door behind herself, and felt, in a sudden rush of unreality, as if she had entered a home where she was a stranger.

She walked into the empty kitchen, dropped her handbag on a chair she had never noticed was quite so red, took out her phone, and dialed Lila's number. She had it because they were technically co-parenting—the boys were with her just now—but she had never once used it before. She wanted to ask Lila something, a question about Martijn and his nature, or about his history and the way he operated. About whether there was something she needed to know that she was missing. She wanted to ask Lila, essentially, what was *happening* with him.

As she heard the phone ring, she realized the absurdity of this mission. What on earth did she think she was going to ask Lila over the phone right now? How would Lila even have an answer? Whatever she knew about Martijn was then, not now. When she heard Lila pick up, Grace clicked END.

Hm. That was a bit of a ridiculous thing to do with everyone on mobile phones, Grace thought. And then there was Lila, calling back.

"Hey, sorry, I picked up just a second too late," Lila said. "Everything okay?"

That was the natural question. Lila and Grace were not likely to converse unless there was some kind of family emergency, and if Martijn was unreachable.

"Oh yeah," said Grace, trying to think fast. "I was just thinking maybe the boys had forgotten…"—she looked around the kitchen for an idea—"their school lunch boxes."

Ugh. The boys were thirteen and fifteen, and had never used lunch boxes. They smeared bread every morning with whatever they were eating that day, liverwurst or filet Americain or slapped on a slice of cheese and stuck it in a paper sack.

"Yeah, no, I don't know," said Lila, confused and, thankfully, distracted. From the sound in the background it seemed as if the apartment over there was full of monkeys. "Hold on." She went away and came back. "Sorry, the delivery company is just in the middle of bringing in Jasper's new bed. Can I call you back?"

"Totally unimportant," Grace said, grateful for someone else's chaos. "No need."

"Okay," said Lila. "All right, then. See you Sunday? Tomorrow."

"Right."

Grace hung up the phone and plopped down onto the closest chair. Jesus, what was she thinking?

It was far too late to ask Lila any questions about Martijn. She'd already committed herself to the man. Anyway, women didn't ask other women about their histories with men, even though that probably would have been the practical thing to do. Of course, the real question wasn't really whether she should have asked Lila all about what Martijn was like in relationships but rather if she would have listened.

Right, time for a bath. She managed to haul herself upstairs to the bathroom, turning on the tub faucet all the way and running the water very hot. *There must be some bubble bath here somewhere,* she thought as she began to unbutton her blouse and kicked off her shoes. She wrestled with her pants until they fell onto the floor and she didn't bother to pick anything up, just left the clothes in a mound on the floor, as if her body had dematerialized suddenly and her costume was all that had been left behind.

And then she glanced up and saw herself in the mirror. The image astonished her. She looked, plainly, awful. Her hair was tousled and unkempt, and her skin was splotchy, with darker continents of melasma drifting across her cheeks, but these signs of aging and personal neglect weren't what concerned her. It was her eyes. She had always had slightly olive-toned half-moons under her eyes, but now they were an unhealthy shade of purple and more deeply sunken. Her eyes, too, seemed somehow dimmed, ransacked of their sparkle.

She pulled out the drawers under the sink and rifled through to find a hand mirror. Tentatively, she raised it and tried to hold it over her shoulder to make a double reflection in the larger wall mirror over the sink. There wasn't enough light in the bathroom to see anything, so she opened the shutters wide and turned on the lights above the sink. Still, it was hard to see. She hoisted herself onto the edge of the sink to get a better look.

Moving the hand mirror like a target, finally she found the right spot. There it was, just below her shoulder blade and above her scapula on the right side of her back. A red spot in the shape of a kidney bean, with a small bloody slice through the middle. It was, in truth, not a bad cut, but it had bled a little. She searched the bathroom drawers for cotton swabs and ran one under cold water, adding soap. She would use it after her bath.

Thinking of how suddenly he'd become so angry that morning, Grace felt it in her bones: something was really wrong. She had to at least try to figure out what.

CHAPTER 7

LADY OF THE FLIES

"Oh, come on!" said Karin, exasperated by the stupidity of Dirk standing there with his giant stick. "Can't we just get going on the trail? I'd like to get to the campsite before *midnight*."

"They're going to have hot chocolate and sausages," added Lotte hopefully.

"Who is going to be the king of the forest?" said Dirk, meaning it. "We're here, no Scout guides for the first time. Now it's just a question of who gets there first."

"Um, no, it's not," said Karin. "This isn't a competition. It's a group activity."

Dirk laughed. "Ugh, group activity." Margot looked at him and laughed too. "So we all walk along in the woods together and get there on time? That's seriously boring. Can't we make some fun out of it? Let's split up and see who makes it there first. Margot and I will give you guys the lead, even."

"Duh, you think we don't know that you're just trying to get rid of us so you can have Margot to yourself?" Lotte said. Karin was again pretty impressed with her. It was cool that she would say those kinds of things out loud. Karin didn't dare to.

"There's no rule that says we all have to go together," Margot said.

"Um, yes, there is," Karin said. "That's actually the first rule. That's the main rule."

Margot crossed her arms over her chest and rolled her eyes. "Well, it's a stupid rule."

"O-M-G, guys," said Lotte. "We don't want to be all alone in the forest; it's getting dark out here, and there aren't any grown-ups. The whole thing is to stay together. Let's just keep going, okay?"

"Okay," said Karin. "Cool. Let's just go."

Dirk leapt into the air and came down from the top of the hill, not far from where Lotte and Karin stood. "You'll have to get through me first!" he said. "That means you'll have to battle me." The giant silver stick came a little too close to Karin's face.

"Jesus, you could've hit me in the head with that," she said. "Quit fooling around."

Dirk's eyes met hers, and they were not friendly. They were darkening into narrow slits. "Why do you think you're in charge, little miss lady? Aren't you the youngest? I'm the oldest," he said. "I'm the fastest, the strongest. I'm also the smartest."

Margot giggled, maybe without meaning to. Karin and Lotte glanced at each other, Lotte rolling her eyes. This was probably not the reaction Dirk expected. "Stop being such a...a...boy," Lotte said. "I'm getting really tired of it."

Without even a pause, Dirk swung the giant stick at Lotte, crying out, "Hack!" She jumped, missing the biggest part of the stick, but one of the smaller branches hit her on the side of the calf. She cried out in pain and grabbed for her leg, falling over. Then Dirk started laughing, like some kind of psychopath.

"Dirk!" cried Karin, but he seemed not to hear.

From the heath, Lotte stared up at Dirk, wildly.

"You jump pretty well," he said. "I'm impressed."

"What the... What is *wrong* with you?" said Karin. "Seriously! That is not at all funny." For a second time, she found herself crouching down beside Lotte. This was so crazy. He was being such a shit.

Karin could not believe it was going like this. She wished so hard that she had her phone so she could call someone and complain. Before she stood up, she decided to try to disarm him. Get that crazy stick out of his hands.

From a crouched position she sprang up, like a frog, her hands out in front of her. She managed to knock him over, probably just because of the surprise of it, and the stick toppled backward onto the ground behind him.

"I'll get it," called Margot, and for a second Karin thought she was going to join the girl team against the crazy boy. But no. A second later Margot was standing holding the butt of the giant silver branch toward Karin like a spear. "Don't you move," she told Karin. "Or I'll..."

She didn't finish her sentence, but Karin didn't think she had it in her to do anything. Margot was pretty athletic, but she wasn't brave—Karin knew that much. She climbed on top of Dirk and tried to jab her elbow into his chest right in the center of his rib cage, where it might hurt. But she had misjudged Margot, who somehow got up the courage to jab the stick right into Karin's butt. "Owww!" Karin cried out, reaching back to touch the place where she'd been wounded. "Fuck! That is so crazy. What are you guys doing?"

Dirk took the opportunity to stand up, while Karin and

Lotte were still on the ground. He stood over the two of them, wiping his hands against each other. "You guys are too easy," he said. "You barely put up a fight." As if it was all just a big joke.

"Why are you being like this?" Lotte almost whimpered from behind Karin. "This is so seriously wrong."

Dirk tried to fake a big yawn. "You guys are so boring," he said. "Come on, Margot, let's just go on our own. They'll figure it out for themselves." And just like that, they took off again, on the trail, over a mound through the purplish heath. Of course neither Karin nor Lotte wanted to follow.

They both sat there on the ground for a few minutes, trying to figure out what had just happened. Karin thought about this book that her mom had given to her to read in English called *Lord of the Flies*. It had given her nightmares. It was about boys deserted on an island after a plane crash, without any adults. They have to fend for themselves, but about half of them were just nasty and caused problems, while the other half tried to get back to civilization, like by sending out smoke signals and stuff like that. But the little kids went missing in the end; the bad kids won. She couldn't quite remember, but was one of the boys killed by the others?

"Do you think he did that just to get alone with Margot?" Lotte asked after some silence.

"Probably," conceded Karin.

"Geez, I would have told them to just go off on their own if they just asked," said Lotte. "Who wants to be with *them* anyway?"

"I know," said Karin. "Exactly."

Karin looked at Lotte's leg, which had a red mark on it

where Dirk had hit her with the branch. "I wish we had some ice for that," said Karin. "My mom would always put ice on it. Or arnica."

"Arnica," said Lotte. "My mom is crazy for that stuff. She smears it on everything." Then she thought. "Oh, I might actually have some in my bag." Lotte scooted herself on her butt across the sand to grab her backpack, which had fallen a while ago. She rooted around and actually found the cream. "That was so weird," Lotte added. "I really can't believe it."

"I know," agreed Karin. "Can you look at my back? Margot really stabbed me with that thing."

Lotte finished putting the arnica on her leg and scooted over a little bit to sit next to Karin, who leaned forward and lifted up the back of her shirt to show Lotte. "Hmm," said Lotte. "It might sting if I put this on."

"Is it bad?" asked Karin.

"I mean, not really," said Lotte. "But we have to tell Rutger or whoever about it later. That's really weird, what they did. Just to get away from us? What do you think they plan to do?"

Karin just shook her head. She literally had no clue. Smoke pot? Have sex? Here, in the forest? That didn't sound at all appealing to Karin.

Truly, Karin could not figure out how Margot could be attracted to Dirk. She did not *get* the whole thing about boys, not really. At school she felt a little flutter sometimes when she passed a certain boy named Isaac, who wore round glasses. But she'd never spoken to him. She'd liked other boys when she was littler, like Jimi in her Group 8 class, who was calm and placid and beautiful, with blue eyes and angelic blond curls. But since starting secondary school this year, she had noticed that other girls were kissing boys and talking to them in a whole new way, and Karin didn't have any idea how to begin doing all of that. She was a little afraid of the whole thing of people touching each other, under the shirt, in their pants—yuck.

What was it with Dirk, though? Karin had kept saying how the whole idea was to work as a team, but then he'd just accused *her* of wanting to "take over." It didn't make any sense.

The girls didn't have to say anything about it anymore. No way were Karin and Lotte going to chase after the other two. They'd just find their own way, with their half of the map. They'd probably make it to the campsite a lot faster than the other two anyway.

Without talking about it anymore, they both got up and brushed themselves off. Lotte pointed toward the trail that seemed to head northwest, not the one Dirk and Margot had taken, obviously. So what if they were just two twelve-year-old girls? They were both pretty smart, and not at all crazy. They were way better off on their own.

CHAPTER 8

ACCOUNTING

Grace, now in Martijn's terry robe, her skin still warm and doughy after a long drench, climbed the stairs and looked up at the door to his office, which was at the top of the house, in a converted attic reachable only by a ladder. It was an A-shaped space with a single window that offered a view across red-tiled rooftops, including the steeple of the church tower, with its bright blue imperial crown. It was a lovely view but one Grace had only ever seen a few times, because Martijn had claimed the room as his private office.

She had been very respectful of the idea of his "man cave"—understanding at a basic level that he might need a space of his own—although it had made her slightly uncomfortable to think that part of their house was off-limits to her. In any case, he kept it so messy that it gave her a headache to even look inside, so she hadn't bothered to make a fuss. He wouldn't even allow the cleaners who came once a month to vacuum in there or to run a duster along the exposed surfaces; he liked to say that it was his "own private pigpen." Fair enough.

Now, though, she looked up at it with a kind of curiosity

that amounted to hunger. Since he wasn't home, she could at least enjoy the view for a few minutes, right?

As she put one foot on the first step of the ladder, she acknowledged to herself that this was an obvious betrayal of trust. He'd explicitly asked that she not go in there. If he found out she had, he would definitely be upset. But despite his admitting it was work that was bothering him, Grace worried he'd change his mind about saying anything more. What if he came back and nothing changed?

Anyway, he was gone for the whole night—and did he need to find out? She could be careful, make sure she didn't really touch anything. Plus, she shouldn't have to be afraid of her husband, right?

So she climbed, putting one foot and then the other on the ladder, until she had to grasp the handle and push up through the trapdoor. Then she hauled herself up into the room. She was immediately hit by a stench of old food, mildew, and—could it be?—cigar smoke. Did Martijn sit up here in the evenings puffing a Cuban? Was that his big secret?

She looked around at the drab office furnishings, the desk with its black Dell desktop computer, a metal filing cabinet from the 1970s, a bookcase with lots of dusty old volumes she was sure he hadn't touched in years. There was a single plant underneath the window, but it was half dead already, poor thing. The only thing that was respectably new in the room was his office chair, an expensive ergonomic model he'd probably purchased with a company discount.

Keeping her little promise to herself, she went to the window first, to catch her glimpse of the view. It was a cloudy night, so she couldn't make out the moon or many stars. She could see the silhouettes of the canal houses, all triangles and pentagons jutting up into the sky at odd angles. Somehow it made her think of being under the water in an ocean of sailboats, seeing only their hulls. It was pretty. It was nice. But it wasn't why she was really here, was it?

Grace took a few steps back and let herself fall into the soft trampoline-like seat of his high-priced chair. She swiveled it back and forth a couple of times, getting a lay of the land. The desk was covered with dark gray three-ring binders stacked on top of one another, many of them bursting with papers. How could a man who was supposed to be a rationalist keep his files in such a chaotic state?

On the spine of each one was written a name, presumably of each of his accounting clients: VELDKAMP; VISSER; VRIES, DE. These were the *V*s. On the other side of the desk was a manila file labeled OPERATIONAL SUPPORT, which seemed to contain nothing but financial spreadsheets. Boring, she thought. Just a lot of boring numbers. This couldn't be what was keeping him up late, what was making him so tense, what was absorbing all his energy, could it? How did he really keep himself occupied up here?

Grace turned toward the filing cabinet, pressed the latch, and pulled out the top drawer. Did he keep his secrets here? A bottle of scotch? A pair of panties? A secret stash of porn? It was ever so slightly titillating to think, for even a moment, that he had a whole erotic life hidden away up here.

But no, Martijn's files, Grace found, were all that filled this cabinet, and they were meticulously orderly and alphabetized. They seemed to be labeled with the names of clients: AARDEN, AUGUSTINE, BEEK, BEYL, BROUWER, CORNELISSEN... alphabetical. Ah, here was the evidence of the rationalist she'd married.

While thumbing through his files, she mused how strange

it was that he basically never talked about his work with her, not ever. What a contrast he was to Pieter, who had so captivated her with his work stories that she'd fallen not really into his arms but into the universe of his job. Well, at least an accountant wasn't someone who would find himself in the crosshairs of a sniper's rifle. Boring, in this case, was safe.

The top drawer stopped at the Gs; she closed it and opened the next, walking her fingers forward through the folder labels to HOOGENDIJK, since one always does seek out one's self. As in Pieter Hoogendijk, since he had been a client. Or in this case, GRACE AND PIETER HOOGENDIJK.

Grace had met Martijn for the first time at Pieter's memorial service. He'd approached her during the reception, seemingly out of nowhere, and pressed his business card into her hand. MARTIJN VAN ROOSENDAAL, it had read. ACCOUNTING. She had looked at the black print on the plain white rectangle, and in her haze of grief had grasped only the spiritual sense of the word "accounting," as in reckoning.

It was in that same bewildered spirit, still lost in grief and seeking answers, that she had dialed the number on Martijn's card a week later at 11 p.m., after hours of weeping, hoping that this mysterious man, shrouded in a very large dark-brown beard with kind green eyes, would somehow help her make sense of what had happened. It hadn't occurred to her immediately, or in any concrete sense, that he was the actual accountant of Pieter's personal finances.

The thick GRACE AND PIETER HOOGENDIJK file she had in her hands now must have been started when Martijn met Pieter, a few years earlier. It certainly looked like a relic of another era, yellow and aged to the point that it seemed like someone had used a lighter to singe its edges. She opened it out of sheer curiosity, not expecting to find anything more surprising than bank statements, notarial deeds, and ancient tax forms.

The first thing that fell out, though, right into her lap, was a photograph of the two of them, her and Pieter, when they were much younger, in South Africa, many years ago. That was funny. What was a photograph from that era doing in Martijn's bookkeeping? She pulled the picture closer to her face to try to figure out what image this was and when it had been taken.

This was an old one, shot long before Karin was born, when they had only just met. Funny—it wasn't one of her photographs, definitely not one of his. They didn't seem to be posing for it, but you could see both their faces pretty clearly, in spite of the wild hair they both had then. This wasn't one of the photos contained in any of their family albums, of that she was sure. Who had taken it?

It was clearly Cape Town, because she recognized the palm trees and the colorful cabins on Muizenberg Beach in the background. She did know exactly where it was taken— not far from one of their favorite bars, actually the place they'd met, a real dive called the Black Swan. Her best guess was that it was taken around that time, 1996. Back then, she'd been twenty-four and met this unruly thirty-six-year-old Dutch photojournalist who spoke with a funny accent and had a million crazy stories, at a bar where she'd gone to listen to jazz.

She recognized her younger self in that picture—what, nearly a quarter of a century ago now?—her hair cropped into a curly bob, with bangs falling into her face. Pieter with his long hair, looking like skin and bones under a T-shirt that hung off him like a tent. Ha. When she'd met him she'd immediately insulted him by saying, "I thought Dutch people were supposed to be tall," to which he'd laughed and explained that stereotypes always had exceptions. He was just barely as tall as she, five foot nine.

But he loomed over her in so many other ways. Pieter was already a veteran war photographer by then, having covered the Iran-Iraq War, the Lebanese Civil War, the bombing of Libya. He'd launched into photojournalism right out of secondary school in Amsterdam, not even nineteen, never gave a thought to university, even though he'd aced all his exams. He'd just gone off with a Leica to Syria during the first Islamist uprising there, on his own. "That was seriously stupid," he confessed to her, twining his fingers with hers at that jazz bar, maybe boldly and too soon. "I almost got killed the first day."

He still had the scar on his belly to prove how stupid he'd been, he told her. Did she want to see it? Yes, he'd been one of those cowboy gonzo photojournalists of the 1980s, fearless, reckless, and ultimately insanely lucky to have made it out alive. How sexy was all of that to her at the time! He talked a mile a minute about war and competing tribes and CIA informants and weapons traders and government complicity and human rights and aid organizations and who was doing what to endanger or save humanity, and to her, back then, everything he said was genuinely, truly fascinating.

Pieter was thirty-eight when they married, two years later, quite a lot older than Grace, and that seemed hard to her at the time. But the years passed, and suddenly she herself was thirty-eight, and she realized that if she wasn't going to have kids with this wild man, she wasn't going to have kids.

Pieter claimed by then that he had mellowed, and he

regretted his youthful bravado, even if he still loved to show off the puncture wounds in his left hip, where he'd gotten grazed by bullets in Libya, or the scar just below his collarbone where he'd been whacked with a Rwandan rebel's machete. She, too, counted herself lucky that he was alive.

And then, after all that, when Karin was ten, he wasn't anymore. All the bad luck he'd managed to sidestep for all those years finally caught him. She'd had Pieter for twenty-two years, and Karin had had him for ten. Those were the numbers.

She looked again at the picture of the two of them from so many years ago. How strange that she'd never seen it before. Who had taken it? And from where? It was blurry, slightly overexposed, and taken from very far away, like someone had photographed them from a moving car across the street. It was grainy, suggesting it had been shot using a long zoom lens. Like someone had been watching them, snapping shots to indicate their whereabouts, locate them. Why would Martijn have this picture?

CHAPTER 9

RED DEER

It was dark now, but more like a deep-sea blue than black. They could see stuff, but more like the outlines of things, and all kinds of crisscrossing shadows that made the forest feel more strange, or maybe magical. It was a bit creepy with the weird gnarled trees that looked just a little like swimmers doing a sidestroke, or swimmers drowning.

Lotte, who was walking ahead of Karin, always started to talk a whole lot when she got nervous, and now was one of those moments. "Where are you going for winter break?" she asked, and said without waiting for an answer, "We're going to Thailand. My parents have been telling me all about it. They've already been there four times. They say we can swim all day long. They have this place that's just a hut with, like, the walls completely open, and they say it gets hot enough that you never want to close the doors or anything."

Karin's family hadn't made any plans for the winter break. Everything was too scrambled at home. She didn't even know if they'd be living in the same house in a week or two, the way it was between her mom and Martijn. "We rented a place in the South of France," Karin lied, remembering a holiday she took with her mom and dad when she was younger. "They got a cottage there, and we can go hiking nearby. My parents like to go wine tasting, and they let me have a few sips. It's really pretty all around there."

Lotte didn't seem to be very interested in this lie, or maybe she just needed to talk. "In Thailand, they have these places where you can go and take care of elephants. You wash them with a hose and feed them with buckets, and if you're lucky, my mom says, you can even ride on one."

Karin remembered the elephants she had seen with her mom and dad at Kruger Park when they'd gone to South Africa that one time together. She'd been really young then, like eight. They'd had to get shots for that trip, and Karin never forgot how much it hurt. But it had been worth it. How giant and graceful the elephants were. So gentle, even though they had so much power; Karin respected that. "My mom went by herself last year, just to see what it was like, and if it was okay for me to go," continued Lotte. "And she said there are a lot of kids who live in the village, and they really like foreigners, like to take them around and show them all the amazing plants and places to swim, and I don't have to be with my parents the whole time, like here..."

The trail here was half paved with asphalt but mostly covered with sandy dirt and overgrown with tufts of grass that sprouted up through cracks. While Lotte talked, Karin tried to convince herself not to be frightened of the coming darkness. She'd been here at night before, and she had never been scared then. But of course that was with her dad, and being with her dad had always made everything okay. He'd let her go off on her own a bit and collect kindling; he even had let her light the campfire and poke it with a branch. The Veluwe had never seemed scary before. But now, with just the two of them, just her and Lotte?

Karin pictured her father here, guiding them, the straps of all his camera bags crisscrossing his broad chest like some kind of special armor. She saw his face, his pale blue eyes, always smiling when he saw her, and his nose, wide and sturdy, and his salt-and-pepper stubble, not thick enough to be called a beard, really. He had on a sort of padded vest with lots of pockets, and that black-and-white-checkered scarf he always wore, which he sometimes used to clean his lenses in a pinch.

"Just a little farther," he had told her, looking back and giving her a wink. "It's just over this ridge."

The first time they'd come here together hadn't been that long after the trip to South Africa. She'd begged to go back to Kruger Park, but her parents said they'd have to save up for another trip. It cost, like, thousands of euros. Her dad said they should start exploring local nature, their own national forests. He was going to learn how to shoot nature photographs because it was safe—safer than Africa. No vaccinations needed!

"Come on, darling," he'd said. "See that big boulder there? That's where we'll stop."

She'd followed him, up over the dune-like hills to a place where there was a rock just big enough to hide them. He dropped his camera bags off his shoulders and sat beside the rock, motioning for Karin to do the same. She slouched over and sat next to him, resting her back against the rock.

"What now?" she asked.

"Now we wait," he said. "We wait for the deer to come."

"When are they coming?" she asked, naturally.

He laughed and put his arm around her shoulders. "They're on the two forty train," he said.

Karin didn't get the joke at first and tried to find the train tracks nearby. "Ha ha, very funny. How long?"

"That's the beauty of it," he said. "The deer are in charge. We're on their schedule now."

"Hm." Karin wasn't sure how she felt about this. Maybe it would be more interesting to be at home, where they had a comfortable couch, and Nickelodeon. Where her mom could make them popcorn while they were waiting. "Can't we put out treats for them or something? I have yogurt bars."

Her father laughed, his eyes flashing with pride. "I guess I've raised a city girl," he said. "But we can still fix that."

Karin didn't like the sound of this. She opened her sequin-covered backpack and took out her journal, to start writing in it.

"That's a good thing to do," said her dad, "but first I want to teach you how to breathe while we're waiting."

"Um, Dad, I already know how to breathe."

"Of course you do, but I'm going to show you how to breathe a special way, so you don't scare the deer away," he said, adding, "so they'll come faster."

Karin put down her journal and pen. "If you think it'll help."

Breathing for deer meant mostly breathing through your nose, really slow and really deep, it turned out. Like what they had to do in yoga classes with her mom. She found it kind of hard. Her dad kept saying, "Even slower." Until she felt like she might actually stop breathing if she slowed down any more. After a while, he told her she'd "mastered it!" So they sat as still as possible and breathed for a while like they didn't exist at all.

They sat there for almost an hour like that. Hidden by the rock, glancing over into a clearing, waiting for the deer and making no sound. But then her legs started to cramp up and she felt like telling her father that she was bored, she wanted to go home. Karin started wiping the dirt off her legs and was getting ready to stand up.

And just as she very nearly revealed herself and ruined everything, she saw it, there in the distance, a single red deer. She crouched back down and tapped her father, who was already snapping away. "That's a hind," whispered her father. "A female. She won't travel alone. There will be more." He added, "If we keep still."

He was right: a few minutes later, another hind came out from the wooded area, and then another and another. "Now, wait for the stag," he said. "He's got to herd his harem."

Karin had to stifle a laugh. "Harem?"

"Shhhhh," her father said gently.

That was also true. There were six or seven hinds grazing around the edge of the clearing when the stag came—a really big deer with a set of giant antlers like a tree on his head. He seemed like a king there. All the hinds glanced up. The antlers were crazy big—like almost bigger than his body—and covered with a soft kind of downy felt that Karin wished she could touch.

"Just wait," her father told her, ever so quietly. Suddenly another stag appeared. He was larger than the first one, but he had only one antler, on the left side of his head. "Drama," her dad whispered as he very slowly put down one camera and picked up another. Karin tried to remember how to breathe, but she found herself gasping.

The second stag let out a roar, like a real roar, like a lion. Karin didn't even know they could do that. Then it kind of jolted up onto its hind legs, to standing, like a man. The first stag jumped up on his back legs too. It was so crazy, like playing chicken. They both used their front legs to whack, to try to knock the other over. They got closer and then locked horns. The first stag, the one all the girls liked, just smashed into the second, the one with the single antler, and knocked him down. He found his footing and got up quickly and started to run off, but his remaining antler just toppled off his head like a fallen crown. Then he disappeared into the woods.

Karin's heart was beating fast. That was nuts, what she'd just seen. She couldn't believe it. In spite of herself, and everything she had been taught, she let out a whooping yell, like her team had won a football match. "Whoaah!" she cried. And of course all the deer looked at her, in a split second, and then instantly, like in a puff of smoke, ran off.

"Karin!" her father had said in a tone of serious disappointment. "You had to?"

Karin's father faded and disappeared in the bushes as she realized that she hadn't heard Lotte's voice in a while. "Lotte?" she called out, looking around and seeing that it was suddenly dark, suddenly really nighttime. That was odd. "Lotte? Lotte don't go too far ahead of me!"

But there was no answer. "Huh?" Karin said out loud, but to herself. Because nobody else was there. "Okay, Lotte, this really isn't funny. It's kind of scary out here. I'm not really feeling like playing games."

Still no answer. The trail ahead was empty, the side-stroking trees around her just as creepy. Behind her, no sign of movement. "Lotte, this is seriously not cool!"

Dead silence.

Why would Lotte run off ahead of her? Or could she have fallen behind? How did Karin lose track of her—just because she drifted off into memories? Where could Lotte have gone? It just didn't make any sense.

There was a curve in the path, and a hill not far from where she was walking. She decide to climb up the slope so that she could get a better vantage. "Lotte? Are you there?" she called out, stepping up a sandy embankment. No answer at all.

She hadn't been going *that* slow. At the top of the hill, she looked out over the landscape, the mounds of earth that looked like sand dunes, the patches of dry grass, the stumpy trees now looking like they were making fists with their fingers. Mean trees. Angry trees in the darkness.

"*Looottttaaaaaa?*" she cried out. "*Hellllloooooo???*" she shouted, her voice singsong, and waited, this time hearing faint reverberations, as if she were calling out inside a cave.

Just like that, she thought. *And just like that, so fast, I'm alone?*

CHAPTER 10

FILE FOLDERS

Grace had held on to Martijn's ACCOUNTING card through Pieter's memorial reception for no particular reason, except that it was something to clutch in her hand so she wouldn't reach for a cigarette. She'd given up smoking when she was pregnant, for good. She'd kept the card in her pocket until she'd arrived at the sad little storefront in a blocky modernist office building to meet Martijn van Roosendaal like a woman in search of a soothsayer.

She had barely noticed the midcentury furniture positioned like building blocks on the slate-gray carpeting or the mousy brunette with the near-bouffant who tried to block her way into Martijn's office. He recognized her immediately, and came out into the hallway to welcome her into his chambers.

"My father founded this accounting firm with his twin brother," Martijn explained once he'd seated her and settled himself again behind a wide oak desk, appearing far more ordinary, and handsome, with his beard shaved off, and not at all like the wise man in colorful silks she'd imagined in her hallucinatory anguish. "I've expanded it into some other areas," he continued, then added more pointedly, leaning forward and looking right into Grace's eyes, "with your husband's help."

Grace felt her heart muscle squeeze and knew a wave of sadness was coming in, like seagulls sensing a storm. "My husband's help," she repeated, but it didn't make sense to her. What help could Pieter possibly have given to an accounting firm?

"I'm sorry, late husband," said Martijn, as if that was the area of confusion. "I want you to know that Pieter was not only a client to me but someone I counted as a dear friend."

Grace didn't know what to do with this information. Pieter had never mentioned a Martijn van Roosendaal to her, and she was sure she'd met all his friends. None of them, as far as she knew, worked in polished faux-vintage offices with glass walls and persnickety receptionists out front. Not a one of them seemed anywhere near so established.

What came out through the subsequent discussion, however, confused her even more—Pieter had accumulated a great deal of wealth in the last year or two, working with Martijn, apparently, and this left Grace and Karin, as Martijn put it, "in a very strong position financially." Martijn was methodical in laying it all out for her, explaining that she only had to sign some papers, here and here, to be able to move the income into her own accounts.

Yes, that was how she'd met Martijn, over financial paperwork, and somehow, over time, they'd fallen in love. Probably a lot of it had to do with his looks, his charm, his apparent eagerness to support the grieving widow, as well as her own desire to make life easier and safer and more, well, normal.

Grace hadn't thought a lot afterward about the idea that

Martijn and Pieter had been "friends." She had assumed it had been an overstatement on his part, perhaps to make her feel more confident. But now, as she rifled through this folder, with the photograph of her and Pieter as young lovebirds, she wondered: was it possible that Martijn had somehow known them without her knowing him? There turned out to be a lot of pictures of the two of them way back when, as well as a copy of Pieter and Grace's wedding invitation from 1998. That was definitely odd. How could she not have known him then?

They'd held the ceremony in the tiny garden of a friend's house in Muizenberg, near the bar where they'd met two years earlier; way too many people were crammed into the space, but there was lots of music. They'd told everyone to bring an instrument, and just as they exchanged rings, the whole backyard filled with cacophonous sound, and there was playing and singing and dancing until dawn. Even if they'd actually known Martijn back then, he would not have fit into that scene.

Grace started to have a strange tickling feeling in the back of her throat, and when she swallowed it seemed like she was trying to digest a big lump of something hard and prickly.

What could be the explanation for this? She pawed through the other documents in the file and saw other artifacts of Pieter and Grace's old life—more discolored photographs of the two of them taken from afar. They were weird pictures, not images she'd ever seen before, and definitely not taken by anyone in her family. There was nothing intimate or familial about them. They again seemed to be pictures taken by someone who was observing them, from quite a distance. Maybe even spying on them. Yes, that was it. "Surveilling" was the word. These seemed to be images taken by a private detective or maybe Dutch intelligence, or even an FBI agent? To what end? For what purpose?

It was, in a word, creepy. Surveillance images of Pieter, and not just of Pieter but also of Grace and even of little Karin when she was just a toddler. Once she understood the unlikely and, well, rather creepy perspective of these images, she started to look at the rest of the paperwork in the file in a different way.

These were records of their whereabouts, lists of times and places of their trips. Obviously trips Pieter had taken for his work—for reporting—but also, it seemed, some family trips. The records continued on through their move to the Netherlands, which had happened just before Grace gave birth to Karin. There was also a photograph of tiny baby Karin in the arms of Grace, with Grace's mother—now long dead. None of these had been taken up close; apparently they had been again taken with a zoom lens, since they too were extremely grainy.

Who had taken these pictures? And why hadn't Grace known about them? Grace remembered that once or twice Pieter had mentioned that he was probably being spied on, and at least once AIVD, the Dutch national security agency, had contacted his newspaper editor about images he'd published possibly compromising state security. But he'd never told Grace that there was an actual file on him.

Beyond all that, what was Martijn doing with this file? Had someone given it to him? And if so, why? What would he have wanted with it?

Her head was spinning—not metaphorically but physically. She had to lie down, and did so in spite of the knowledge that insects of the netherworld definitely dwelled in the coarse threads of this rug. She lay still and kept her eyes closed for a moment to try to stop the rotation, and then opened them when it didn't stop. She looked up and tried to anchor her vision to the ceiling beams. That worked better. She'd come up here looking for answers but had found only reasons to ask more questions.

Okay, she thought, there must be a perfectly logical explanation for what she had found. Maybe Pieter had somehow gotten his hands on his own AIVD or FBI file—people could request those these days, couldn't they?—and he'd just given it to Martijn, his accountant, for safekeeping. After all, he trusted his accountant with his money—and also his history, like a kind of human safe-deposit box. Wasn't that what had attracted Grace to Martijn too? His sense of solidity and safety, a rock in a constantly fluctuating sea? Both of them had latched on to him for that reason.

Her eyes stayed fixed on two particularly large ceiling beams that looked like something taken from a seventeenth-century seafaring vessel. They probably had been stripped from a seventeenth-century seafaring vessel. All these houses, probably all the buildings in the city, were built with repurposed materials from old ships.

Grace took a deep breath. It wasn't such a big deal, any of this, right? Anyway, how did it relate to what was going on with Martijn and her now? Did these pieces even belong to the puzzle she was trying to put together, about what was going on in their own marriage? They seemed like they were puzzle pieces thrown together from two totally different boxes. Both strange. But probably wholly unrelated.

None of this mattered for the moment. This couldn't be what he was hiding. Maybe his secrets could be found on his computer. That was where people lived these days, wasn't it? Anything he was hiding would be there.

She stood up, closed the filing cabinet, and moved to the desk. The keyboard was, of course, filthy. She looked around and saw a box of Kleenex on the windowsill and pulled out some tissues to wipe the keyboard down. To her surprise, the motion of her hand across the keys sparked the computer to life. The screen turned on, brightening the now darkened room.

Huh, thought Grace, who had naturally assumed he would've shut it down before he left. There it was, the computer already booted up and the home screen lit, and there was Martijn's user name, already filled in, in one box, and a flashing box that was just asking her to fill in his password.

Password, thought Grace. *Password.*

Grace was privy to some of Martijn's passwords. His kids' names, his uncle's name, his birthdate. She typed in several variations of those. None of them worked, but if he was trying to conceal something from her, that was no surprise. He'd obviously use a password that she didn't know. She secretly hoped that wasn't the case—then it would be clear that he had nothing to hide. From her, at least.

The computer rejected her attempts, repeatedly. She tried again and it shut her out, locking down so she had to wait for some minutes to try again.

What on earth could his password be? How could she ever figure it out? She rifled around the desk for clues; there must be a Post-it note somewhere around here where he'd scribbled it down to remind himself. Martijn didn't have such an amazing memory. But no, she didn't find anything right in front of her, nothing in any of the usual places someone might keep a password. Anyway, since he used this computer all the time, he would remember it.

She sat back and thought for a moment—how could she unlock Martijn's mind. She thought about what he thought about. She'd already covered Frank and Jasper, Lila, all with numbers and icons. He often used 44 and ** as additions where characters and numbers were required, so it was logical he'd use those here too. She'd hopefully tried Grace and Karin, thinking maybe he occasionally thought of them when he was holed up in here. No. Those hadn't worked either. She remembered Martijn's long-deceased mother's name, Hylke, and wrote that down, and his last name, Van Roosendaal, and then decided to try words about things he liked: "accounting," "coffee," "AFC Ajax," "Westworld."

When the computer allowed her to try again she attempted all of those. No, no, no, no. And then it shut her out again for a full minute. Grace stood, tapping the eraser side of the pencil on her forehead to try to get her brain working. How ridiculous it was to attempt to figure out someone's password when it could be literally anything.

She moved in circles, thinking about what made Martijn tick, what words stuck close to his memory, what kinds of ideas were part of his personal lexicon. It came to her, a sardonic and strange thought, which she almost didn't allow herself to think.

The moment the computer allowed her to try once more, she leaned over and typed it in, thinking it was just a stupid fantasy. As soon as the cursor started blinking, she typed it:

"Pieter," adding a "44" for good measure.

Bingo! She was in.

CHAPTER 11

INLAND BEACH

Karin was trying to "locate" herself, as her father had taught her. She was standing in the middle of a large sand drift, with echoing ridges of white sand that, in places, looked like high waves, frozen at the moment when a surfer would ride them. She had half of the map in her pocket but not the half that showed this spot. Still, she knew the layout of the park well enough to know that to get to the campsite she had to head northwest. Wherever that was.

The compass was what she needed. But where was it? It wasn't in her jacket pocket, where she was sure she had put it last. She had searched through her backpack, knowing already that it wasn't there, and of course did not find it. Could it have fallen out of her pocket when she had the tussle with Dirk on the trail? That was just messed up. She was without a map or a compass.

Now that the sun was down she couldn't use that as a guide either. The sky was really cloudy, so it was hard to see the stars too. She sat herself down on a cushion of green moss on one of the dunes and tilted her head back. Was that it? No, that must be a plane. She tried to find a spot without clouds where she could look. There—that must be it. Or was that Saturn?

Well, she'd call that one the North Star. Maybe it wasn't, but it was her best guess, 'cause it was all she could actually see. So if that was north, then that must be northwest, down this dune, over that sand drift, near where that huge downed tree was. She could get there. But she also knew it was going to be farther than it seemed.

Her father had told her that these sand drifts in the Veluwe were "rare outcroppings" for an inland landscape. High dunes nowhere near the sea. He'd said they were ancient to this forest, dating to the Ice Age. Really super-early farmers may have caused these sand drifts by destroying the land, by tearing up the soil. "Wow, people have always ruined, like, everything," Karin had said at the time. Her father had laughed in that proud way he had. "Well, not everything," he said.

It was really fine sand, and as she tried to walk across it, she kind of felt like her feet were being swallowed up. It was step, sink, and lift. Step, sink, and lift. But she could handle it. She had strong hockey legs. It would just take time.

She knew the names of some of the things around her, and to comfort herself, she tried to remember them. She liked the word for the soft dewy green moss that covered the rocks in the sand drifts: "maidenhair." That one sort of made her blush. And she remembered the name of all the lacy-looking stuff that grew on bark and stones: "lichen." The forest she needed to hike through to get to the campsite was called De Plijmen. She could see the dense, dark tangle of trees from here, as a cluster of shadows. Due west in the Otterlose Forest was where the Scout leaders would be with their tents.

As she walked, she couldn't help but notice dark rain clouds moving in from the direction she was headed. The more she watched, the darker they seemed to become, and they were sort of building up on each other, like, well, a building. *Oh no*. It was just one thing after another, wasn't it?

Where was she going to hide from a storm in the middle of the sand drift? If she had time, she might be able to run around and find some dry wood and make a tiny shelter. But that seemed out of her league, and she'd have to do it fast. Her best bet was to run as quickly as she could into the surrounding forest, at least get some cover from trees. Walking was already hard—but running?

Fighting back the urge to start crying—she didn't have time now, with those clouds moving in—she took off her backpack again and tried to find anything she could use as a tent. The adults had taken the real tents to the campsite so the kids wouldn't have to carry them on their hike, but now Karin thought about what a stupid plan that was. What if something like this happened?

She dug around in her bag until she felt the emergency yellow rain poncho she had put in the bottom. It was thin but water resistant and long enough that it would work as a tarp if she could find some way to prop it open over her. Now the real question was, should she make a run for it? Or should she stay put?

Karin wondered what her father would do. They'd waited out many a rainstorm in the park together, but usually in the car, which was often not so far from their tent. And what had the Scouts taught her about what to do during foul weather? Hm. The main thing she could remember was to try to stay close to the other Scouts, use a tarp, and huddle in a circle to keep warm. That advice wasn't much use now. Karin decided to make a run for it. The edge of the forest didn't seem that far away; she might even make it before the downpour.

She put her backpack on again, stood up, threw her oversized rain poncho over her head, over her jacket and backpack, so the hood rested on her forehead but the rest of it was like a cape, flying out behind her. She held on to the bottom of it with both hands. Then she backed up a few steps, took a running leap, and flew off the side of the sand drift.

She felt the first drops of rain fall on her head, heavy like pennies. Oh no. She looked up to see that the sky was almost completely black. Karin ran. She ran as fast and as far as she could, feeling her feet slip under her with each step, the distance between herself and that shadowy line of trees becoming ever so slightly shorter. She ran and ran as the rain began to pelt her from above, at first feeling every drop that hit her, and then the wind whipped up to turn the rain into an onslaught.

When she reached the edge of the forest and found a tree wide and dense enough to harbor her, she sank down along its trunk and pulled the poncho close around her. Exhausted, terrified, alone in the woods, and not even yet thirteen years old, she thought; Karin began to cry, the tears rolling down her soaked face and mingling with the raindrops to make her face a wet mess.

As she was sniffling and wiping her nose with the soaked sleeve of her jacket, she was startled by the sound of footsteps somewhere behind her. She turned, hardly able to make out anything but the outlines of a form, looming above her, in the shadows of the forest.

"Lotte?" she said, hopefully.

"What are you doing here?"

It was a deep, raspy, scary voice coming from a clump of trees behind her. Definitely not Lotte. All she could see was the shape of a person, a big outline in black. Male or female, she couldn't tell. He or she was definitely bigger than Karin. And it wasn't someone she knew.

She managed to reach into the small front pocket of her knapsack and grab her key chain, which had a mini flashlight dangling on it. She pressed the button and flashed it up into the face of whoever it was.

"Sorry, I am not trying to freak you out," she announced as she did it. "I can't see you."

She didn't mean to startle whoever it was standing there in the clump of trees, but they immediately jumped back like she'd hit them with a dart. Then she waited. *Oh yikes.* What if it was someone horrible? She waited again until she heard the sound of feet clomping on wet leaves. It didn't sound like just two feet. There were more.

The beam of her key-chain flashlight was too small. She waved it in front of her face, hoping to catch sight of something, but all she could see were shadows. And still the footsteps came closer. Then, somehow, she shined it in the right place and found a face. Except it wasn't really a face. It looked more like a horrible mask: it was yellowish white with this big purple mouth that drooped at both sides. She moved the tiny flashlight beam to see better: big eyes too wide surrounded by really dark circles and all these red welts on the face. It was a ghoul out of a storybook.

Karin screamed, and the key chain dropped out of her hands because they were trembling so much. She heard the ghoul yelp at exactly the same time, again like they'd been bit. They leapt away from her once more. She screamed again, until all she could hear was her own scream.

CHAPTER 12

PASSWORD

Grace sat back down at the desk in front of Martijn's computer and marveled. The password alone was bizarre. Why was Martijn so focused on her deceased husband, who could no longer present any kind of threat to him at all? It didn't make sense. If there was something to be concerned about, then why hadn't he talked to her about it—really discussed it with her? They were in a marriage. It couldn't just be insecurity, could it? That seemed just too odd.

Now that "Pieter" had granted her access, Grace could see everything of Martijn's in front of her: all his documents were open, all his browser tabs, all his spreadsheets, and even his contacts. But what did she want to know now? What was she actually looking for?

Since "Pieter" had gotten her this far, she decided to plug his name into the hard drive search bar. Suddenly, a whole series of files popped up on the screen, one after another, like a fan. The first group of them were Excel spreadsheets, with Pieter's name at the top. The titles of these documents read: "Pieter Hoogendijk Photo Series 345," "Pieter Hoogendijk Photo Series 446," and one had a title that included a parenthetical that Grace found particularly mysterious:

"Pieter Hoogendijk Photo Series 525 (code name: Oranje)."
Oranje. Orange—the color of the Dutch state, the House of Orange.

What was that supposed to mean?

Grace clicked on that file and opened the spreadsheet. She could tell instantly that it was a list of images. Grace knew Pieter well enough to understand his method of keeping track of his pictures. It was a little old-fashioned—she knew that these days photographers had more sophisticated means of searching their files—but this was his. He'd write the image number, "IMG 4012," for example, next to the file name, the camera (Pentax or Canon or Canon Wide), the location (such as Johannesburg), the date, and then a little description of the subject: "bus ride." Because she had been working on a book that combined her observations of post-apartheid South Africa with Pieter's photographs, she knew this system intimately, and understood that "bus ride" meant the photos he shot of the early 1990s bus desegregation process, a series of photos he'd actually shot for *Time* magazine.

So for some reason Martijn had a whole lot of Pieter's photo spreadsheets on his computer. She was starting to feel less and less surprised by the strangeness of this fact. But the more she clicked through the spreadsheets, the more she noticed that most of these files were fairly recent, from the period when he was in Syria, near the end of his life. Grace was less familiar with this work. During that time, Grace had been fairly well preoccupied with her own work at home, keeping life moving steadily ahead for Karin, who had been about eight or nine years old at the time, while also holding down her own nearly full-time job for an NGO.

Maybe because Syria was the last place he worked before

he'd been killed, it was the part of his career she kept at a bit of a distance. Since she had never been to the country herself, it also seemed more of an abstract war to her than what they'd experienced together in South Africa in the '90s.

But now she looked more closely at these files, reading the descriptors on the photos. "IMG 3459, Syria, 2013, Al-Mezzeh military hospital." "IMG 3460, Syria, 2013, Al-Mezzeh military hospital, bodies," "IMG 3461, Syria, 2013, Al-Mezzeh military hospital, torture victim." The list went on like this for a while. These were the images he had taken in the hospital that the Syrian government had used as a torture center, Grace knew. He'd managed to get access through a forensic photographer who worked for the regime, but the activity had put them both at tremendous risk. After he'd shot only a couple of rolls, he had to flee the country, or he would have become a victim of the regime himself. Later, the forensic photographer made it out of Syria, smuggling his own images with him. But that was much later.

Grace remembered how Pieter was when he came home from that trip to Syria in 2013. He had come in the door, looking as pale as a ghost, kissed and hugged her and Karin, and gone immediately into the guest bedroom, pulled down the blackout curtain, and slept for three days. She'd been afraid that he was gravely ill. He would only allow her to bring him soup and sit with him briefly. When she did, he would touch her face lovingly and then start to cry, begging that she let him just go back to sleep for a while. She did.

It had been traumatic for her too. She didn't know what he had seen or how it had affected him, and she was concerned that this time it would leave permanent, but invisible, scars. Even later, when he had recovered and he came out and became his easygoing self again, he didn't share with Grace what had happened. She had understood his struggle to communicate—extremely unusual for Pieter: he just hadn't wanted to put it into words.

Only a few of the photographs he'd taken from that trip made it into the main media outlets, she remembered, and he had been dispirited when he was told the others were just too gruesome. The truth of what was happening needed to be told. But that was the irony about the media. The old maxim "If it bleeds it leads" didn't apply if it got too bloody. There were rules at "family" news outlets about how much blood was suitable for publication, and these images, she came to understand, far exceeded those limits.

The truth was, Pieter hadn't even wanted to show Grace these images, even though she had developed a pretty strong stomach for horror over the years. He had said they really needed to be shared with the International Criminal Court in The Hague, so someone could take some action. They were maybe beyond the scope of what public outrage alone could accomplish. Through a good old friend she knew at the court, Jenny Lentiner, an American who worked for the Office of the Prosecutor, she'd managed to put Pieter in touch with the right authorities. Things had moved forward from there.

But once again Grace sat in this office in an ergonomic chair in complete bewilderment. This was old news, Pieter's old work, serious stuff, but yes, personal and private, and, eventually, classified material. What was it doing on Martijn's computer? Why did Martijn have Pieter's Excel sheets? What was he doing, or what had he done with them?

There had been a knot in her stomach all day, and now it started to ache, to burn. She was hit by the terrible reality that she was married to a man she did not know. What role had Martijn played in Pieter's life before he died, beyond working as his accountant? How long had they known each other, before Grace found out that he knew him at all? Even if Martijn had somehow been granted these images by Pieter, say for safekeeping—giving him the benefit of the doubt—why would Pieter have trusted Martijn, and not her, his wife, with that task?

What was also strange was that the lists of the photographs had popped up, but the images themselves hadn't. Maybe somehow they weren't labeled under Pieter's name? Maybe they were filed elsewhere? She tried clicking the photo app, to see what was there. Up jumped a whole slew of images she knew: pictures of Martijn's boys growing up, images of his family with Lila, pictures of Grace and Martijn on trips to holiday-destinations, images from their wedding, photos of all of them together—the new blended family of five.

Okay, that was comforting. That was what should be on this computer, she thought. Somehow she had landed back at normal.

Then she gave it a little more thought. That code name used in one of the Excel sheets. *Oranje*. That was it. Why not try that one instead?

She typed it into the search engine: *"Oranje."* And wham! Thousands of images started piling onto the screen like a deck of cards thrown down on a blackjack table.

These, she knew instantly, were all the images Pieter had never wanted her to see: dead bodies, hundreds of them, strewn across cold concrete floors. Bodies wrapped in plastic, emaciated, stripped naked, and beaten. There were close-ups of individual bodies, with burns the shape of stove elements, strangulation lines on necks, gashes from whippings, limbs hacked and mutilated. The pictures were tossed at her by the computer, one after another, filling up the screen, photo file after photo file. Horror after horror after horror.

Grace, stunned and whiplashed, pushed herself back from the computer as if it, on its own, were trying to attack her. She closed her eyes and breathed deeply, feeling her heart gallop. This was too much. This was not what she had been seeking.

Once her heart had slowed, after the onslaught had faded a bit and she could tell herself that it was "just pictures," she opened her eyes again.

She remembered what Pieter had told her after he'd finally emerged from their darkened guest room after three days of fitful rest. He'd reached out to her and put his hand lightly on her forearm. "They were torturing them all," he had said. "To death."

CHAPTER 13

GHOUL CAMP

"I'm sorry!" Karin cried out. "I'm really sorry. I don't want anything from you. I didn't mean to come here. I'll go away. If you let me be, I'll go away. Please don't hurt me!"

She began to tremble so much that it was crazy. She had no idea what was happening to her. Her hands were all wet, and now her teeth began to chatter, like, really hard. The flashlight wasn't anywhere anymore. It was gone in the dirt. She felt around to find it. *Shit, shit, shit.*

She pulled her knees to her chest and ducked her head, trying to curl up into a tiny ball, like a pill bug. Maybe if she just hid inside her giant rain poncho it would go away.

The bushes around her were making noise again, and there were more of them. The footsteps in the leaves were moving slowly, gently, toward her again. They weren't going to leave her alone.

One of them hovered over her, making her think of a bat. She could hear its breathing, which was not healthy, more like a wheeze. She didn't dare look up and into its face again. She tried not to move a muscle, but her body continued to shake, and she couldn't stop it. "Please, please," she whimpered quietly, to herself. "Please, please, please."

A minute later, another one came and stood over her. They were coming out of the woods. They started to surround her. Their feet were moving in the sodden leaves, crunching and sloshing. Could they be animals? Maybe wild boars? Other night creatures? They weren't animals, and they seemed bigger, wider, more frightening than humans.

"It's a kid," she heard one of them say, and thought, *At least that sounded like a human voice.*

"What's she doing here?" said the voice she had already heard. Raspy, deep.

She felt someone kick her leg with a heavy boot. She whimpered, "Please don't hurt me. Please don't hurt me. I am just a kid. I'm only twelve...I'm here on a dropping."

"A dropping?" She heard laughter—four or maybe five people. They were humans. Just really weird humans. "Like with Scouts?" They continued to laugh.

Karin thought maybe they would leave her alone now, but she felt another kick, this time hard, against her thigh. "Get up," a voice ordered. This time it was a woman's voice. "I said, get up," the woman repeated, before she had even had a chance to move.

"Okay, okay," said Karin, trying to move her legs but finding them stiff. She unfolded her hands, which she had been using to clutch her hood over her head, and reached out to find the ground so that she could push herself up.

Did she have anything she could use to fight them off if they tried to hurt her? Anything sharp? Or long? Or even bright? Losing the flashlight on her key chain meant she'd lost her keys too. Her mom would be mad.

"I'm getting up," she said as she pushed herself up to standing. She felt tiny in their company, all these big bats. "I dropped my keys," she said, knowing that it sounded kind of pathetic. "I dropped my keys in the leaves and I can't find them."

Nobody answered her. She let them see her face, hoping that if they saw she was only a kid they might take some pity on her. Then she could see them a little better. They weren't bats. They were all just wearing big, wide rain ponchos, which covered their whole bodies. All the same. But when she looked closer she realized they weren't rain ponchos, they were just big black garbage bags with holes cut in them for their arms and heads.

"What are you doing out here by yourself?" one of them asked. It wasn't like he wanted to help her to safety. It sounded like he was accusing her of doing something wrong.

"I . . . I . . . g-g-got separated from my . . . my Scout group," Karin stammered through a tight jaw.

"That was stupid. It's pretty dangerous out here."

"I just lost my group, like, a few minutes ago. I'm sure they're right up there, right ahead of me. I'll bet they're waiting for me. I'd better get with them or they'll start to worry."

The one who'd been talking most recently reached out and grabbed her roughly by the arm. "No," she said. "You'll come with us." Oh no, they weren't nice. They were going to hurt her.

All of a sudden they were all talking, and one of them was trying to pull her rain poncho off, and another one was trying to get her backpack out of her hands. Another one said, "Give me that," and basically ripped it away from her. "My backpack . . ." Karin said weakly while one of them held it and another one zipped it open. "It's just my camping equipment," she said.

While some of them went through her bag, a couple of the others walked a little bit away and she could hear them arguing about whether to leave her or take her with them.

Karin blurted out, "If you let me go, I promise not to tell anyone anything! I swear I'll just go my own way and I won't say a word. You can have everything in my backpack. I'll just go."

"Come on," said the one who took hold of her arm, jerking her forward. She wasn't expecting it, and she slipped on the wet leaves, almost falling. "I'm not taking any chances."

Once that one had made up her mind, it seemed like the discussion was over. They were taking her, and no one was going to argue about it anymore. They marched her deeper into the forest, away from where she needed to go, she knew. Karin could tell as much by the smells around her: the deep scent of wet soil and earthworms and drenched bark, like her dad had taught her. She wished she hadn't dropped her mini flashlight. It was a small thing, but she really needed that.

The one by her left arm was holding her tight, and the one by her right arm seemed to be giving her some slack and walking a little behind. She could hear the *swoosh-swoosh* of all their garbage-bag rain ponchos as they walked. Why would anyone wear garbage bags when you could buy a whole rain suit at HEMA for ten euros? Were they just homeless people or what?

"You shouldn't be out here alone," the one on the right said, like he was trying to protect her.

"That's really okay," she said. "I've been in this forest, like, a million times with my father before I was even ten years old. I know how to find my way by the stars. I can light a fire without matches."

It was a pretty dense part of the woods. They were not on a bike trail or even a real walking trail, just a very narrow dirt path that someone had made recently. These people, obviously.

"You're twelve and you know how to start a fire without matches?" said the one on her right. "I'd like to see that."

"Why don't you just shut up and stop talking nonsense," the one on the left said.

Karin smelled something really rank all of a sudden. It kind of hit her smack in the face. Something she had never really smelled before—it was acidic and sharp in her nose. She automatically stopped and almost retched right there in the woods.

"Come on," said the one on her right, jerking her arm with force to make her keep up.

"I'm coming," said Karin. She couldn't understand why no one else seemed to be smelling what she smelled. "Is this where we're going?"

Karin figured it was too late now. They had her. She might as well look. It was a really creepy place. There were these big metal canisters dumped all over the ground, and lots of empty plastic bottles and buckets. But also a crazy number of empty beer bottles all around. Were they drunks, like the sad, red-faced guys who hung out by the corner near her school?

There was some kind of beat-up old caravan covered by a large dark-green tarp that hung from the branches of a twisted tree. This was their place, their, uh, compound? Could they be, like, in some kind of cult? As they got closer, she could see there was also a dark-blue tent.

She tried to keep breathing normally as they dragged her forward. But it was really gross, like putting your face into kitty litter but without the fake flowers or whatever it is they use to make kitty litter smell "fresh." Just cat pee, and really strong. How long would they force her to stay here and what would they do to her?

Just as they reached the camp, the garbage-bag-poncho people all started talking at once. Karin could make out only bits and pieces of the conversations they were having in more than one language. One voice was louder and clearer than all the rest. "What do you expect we can do with her?" she heard her saying. "You think we'll ransom her? Jesus. She doesn't *look* like she comes from money."

They didn't seem normal—well, obviously—but their bodies all seemed to be crooked, or limping, or just kind of bent, and the little she could make out about their forms under the garbage-bag ponchos made her realize that all of them were really skinny. Maybe they were ghouls, or actual zombies—living dead. Vampires?

The one with the loudest voice started cursing. "What the fuck are we going to do, then? You guys are all such fucking idiots! Sometimes I can't even believe it." Suddenly, that one was standing in front of her and pulling back the hood of her poncho, to look more closely at her face.

In spite of herself, Karin looked up, and the sight was freaky. This ghoul's face was like one of those time-lapse apps where you take a picture of a kid and see what they're going to look like when they're really old. But it still kind of looks like the young person, except their skin is all loose and flappy.

Even though she didn't mean to, Karin stepped back, and the ghoul moved closer, leaning over her. Her breath was totally gross, like rotting fish. "You're afraid, aren't you?" she said, and then laughed.

Karin, who totally didn't get the joke, decided to do what her mom always told her to do: "If you can't figure out the right move, just be honest." Nodding her head, slowly, she said, "Yes. You're...you're all scaring me. I'm, like, a little kid," she added. "I'm supposed to be on a camping trip. I really don't want to be here."

The leader laughed again. She had all these missing teeth, which made her look really old, like some kind of cartoon hag. "Of course you're scared," she said to Karin. "We must be fucking frightening." She looked around at the rest of the group, in a semicircle behind her, and they all started laughing.

"Listen," the hag said, "we aren't going to fuck with you because that would be fucking insane and we are not going to be fucking insane, right? We're a bunch of screwed-up assholes, and we've done a lot of bad shit. We've ruined our own lives, yeah, but we're not that fucked up. We're not messed-up humans. We're not going to fuck with a kid."

Karin couldn't even begin to count the number of swear words she'd just been allowed to hear. If her mom was here, she'd go bonkers. At home, if Karin used a single curse word she had to apologize and replace "shit" with "shoot." She just gaped.

"She can build a fire without matches," the guy at her right said, totally randomly. "I'd like to see that."

"Duh, that is so seriously stupid," said the hag. "You want to blow up the entire forest?"

The guy looked hangdog. "I don't mean *right* here. Over there, on the other side of the stream, maybe? I mean, if we're going to be out here in the woods, it would be kind of cool to have a campfire."

Then all of them were talking at the same time again,

arguing about whether or not they could build a fire. Karin was totally amazed. These ghouls were so creepy, but then the one on the right was like a little kid who had never had a campfire before.

"It's not so hard," Karin offered. "I can show you all how to do it. It's pretty easy. I have a tinder kit in my backpack, if you'd let me..." She was starting to be hopeful that she might be able to get her stuff back.

One of them, who looked a little bit older, pushed her way to the front of the group. "Jesus, you're all wet. You got drenched in the rain." She turned back to the others. "She must be cold. We could go across the stream," she said, turning back to Karin, "and you can make your fire there. Anyway, you better stay here with us until the morning. It's not safe for you to be out here."

Some of the other ghouls suddenly seemed all happy. "Yeah, you better stay with us," said another one, and then they were all nodding, except the hag.

The thought of staying with these ghouls, these zombies, these vampires, was crazy, but her dad had said that staying wet when the temperature drops is one way to get sick. "It's really pretty easy to make a fire if you have enough kindling," she said.

And that was how Karin got the ghouls to go out in their garbage-bag raincoats to look for twigs in the forest across the stream from their compound. Since there was a lot of damp wood and brush, she had to show them how to pick kindling from underneath a top layer of logs and leaves. They only let her get her tinder kit after they'd dumped her backpack out onto the dirt, and the tinder was totally soaked. She couldn't use it. But she managed to find a dead birch tree that was still partly standing, and she peeled away the outer bark to find some dry bits inside that were perfect for tinder. Then she used the magnesium rod from her kit. It wasn't like doing it from flint and stone, but still, they were impressed.

Once she'd got it going, she added the sort of damp twigs, which caught pretty well too. Then they all gathered around it. It was almost like a dropping, but with everyone wearing weird, ugly masks. She wasn't totally sure they wouldn't push her into the fire and burn her alive—but she did manage to relax just a little. Sparks flew into the night sky. The smell was comforting, and the crackling sound it made reminded her of all the campfires she'd ever made with the Scouts and with her dad. Her clothes even started to dry. Could she really stay and spend a night here? It was pretty clear they weren't going to return her stuff. What if she wanted to leave? Would they let her?

CHAPTER 14

SPOOKED

Okay, there had to be a hundred good reasons why Martijn would have all this material on Pieter, right? Well, at least one workable reason. That was all there needed to be: one reasonable explanation.

Maybe it was connected to this so-called friendship they'd had that she was never privy to, Martijn as an invisible man in her life all along. Could it be that his interest in her went far beyond her and to Pieter—or rather, somehow *through* Pieter? Or was she going a little bit mad now, trying to get this all figured out in her head? There had to be a simpler explanation.

She should just ask Martijn what it was all about, shouldn't she? After all, they were married, husband and wife. They were supposed to trust each other and talk things out. She should ask him about things before she jumped to conclusions. She owed him the respect of asking, right?

Grace paced. First she paced in Martijn's attic office. Then she climbed down the ladder, with the intention of going to her room. Next she paced up and down the hallway between the bedroom and the bathroom. She pulled at strands of her hair; she stared at herself in the mirror, as if that would provide answers. She became so tangled up in her head that she screamed into the toilet.

Okay, she would do two things. First, she would pack. Because she had to get out of here. No matter what was going on with this, she was truly frightened of Martijn. Who was he? And had he ever loved her?

She would pick up Karin from the dropping and then she'd take her to a hotel for a few days and they would figure out whatever the hell was going on from there. Maybe it was nothing. Maybe they would have a brief vacation, enjoy a few museums, and come home and everything would be all right, normal.

The other thing she would do was call Martijn, because that was what a non-hysterical, non-bewildered person would do when they came across confusing information. They would ask in a calm, reasonable way: *"Hey, what's all this about?"* Yes, that was what she would do too, because she was calm and reasonable. And she would make that call just as soon as she found herself to be in a calm enough state to make the call. She would. First, though, she would pack.

It was hard to know what to pack when your head wasn't attached to your body. Grace's head seemed to be floating above her, like a kind of drone, looking down on her life, taking inventory, and trying to make sense of it all. She was just a single piece in a giant puzzle, and the pieces were scattered all over the place.

Martijn was her husband, the man she shared a bed with every night, and whom she kissed on the lips and told about her day and shared the details of her daughter's life. Her home, this house, was a place where she filled wooden bowls with fresh fruit for everyone to eat, where she made sure that each child's bed had the same matching, paisley-patterned bedsheets that were non-offensive to any age group, and a yoga nook where there were soft meditation cushions and brass chimes and sculptures of Buddha in case anyone ever felt they needed a time-out.

And yet it was also a place where, upstairs, in a private chamber at the top of the house that she was strictly forbidden to enter, her husband held a collection of information about her former, murdered husband that suggested—perhaps only circumstantially, certainly only circumstantially so far—that, in the extreme worst-case scenario, he was some kind of secret agent or operative or Syrian government spy who had been tracking her husband's movements. And what if she was right about any of this crazy absurdity? Could he have been involved in Pieter's death?

No, it couldn't be true. None of it could be true. It simply didn't make any sense. Oh, how he would laugh at what she was imagining! How he would hold his belly and laugh at the hilarity of it all. Yes, of course he would be just a little bit irked that she had gone through his stuff and drawn conclusions based on some random bits of information. But he would be sensible about it.

Grace started grabbing clothes off the hangers in her closet and just stuffing them into a suitcase lying on her bed. It didn't matter what she brought with her, as long as it would serve as clothing. Then she went over to her bureau and seized handfuls of underwear and socks from the top drawer, remembering to take a pair of pajamas and the small box of her mother's pearls hidden in the back. One after another, she yanked out the drawers and pulled out jeans, pants, shirts, sweaters, and just threw them into her suitcase.

Grace had a fleeting sick feeling in the pit of her stomach. What if her suspicions would prove to be correct? That was the most chilling prospect.

There was enough in this suitcase. She zipped up one side and then tried to zip it closed all the way. There was too much in there, though, and it wouldn't quite shut. She got up on the bed and sat on the top of it and forced the suitcase to close, and now it did, and she zipped it up while sitting on top. Then she pressed his number and waited. The phone rang only three times before he picked up.

"Honey?" he said. Already that relaxed her. "I'm surprised to hear from you."

Grace let out a soft giggle, a girlish habit of hers that she couldn't shake. She laughed whenever she was nervous. "Yeah, I know. I didn't think we'd need to talk till you were back tomorrow, but something came up."

"You missed me?" Martijn said hopefully.

Grace, so ready to be assuaged, took this as a comfort.

And then, more formally and brusquely, "What's up?"

Grace was still sitting on the suitcase, bouncing ever so slightly. "Um," she said, and then there was a long pause. "I went into your office. Please don't be mad. I know you really like to have your own private space, and I respect that. I was just hoping to clean it up while you were gone. I was going to surprise you by making it really tidy for when you came back. Wow, it really did need a vacuum, honey."

There was silence on the other end of the line. All she heard was breathing, deep and long inhales and exhales, that almost sounded like he was not actually paying attention, like he was hauling something over there. Like he was dragging something across the ground.

"Sorry, come again?" he said.

He had not been listening. She repeated herself, nearly word for word, trying to sound even more cheerful and nonchalant than before. "Hm, that's thoughtful of you," said Martijn, sounding like he wasn't exactly buying her act but willing to go along with it for the sake of—something. "I can clean it myself if I want it tidier." He paused. "But I appreciate the sentiment."

They were both silent for a moment. How far were they going to extend this particular theatrical performance? If he was trying to hide something, he would probably start feeling worried right now, right?

"I just kind of got curious and I found something—well, I found something I thought was surprising..." There was really no way to make it sound like she had stumbled on this material. Oh, why had she called him? She should have just waited until he came home and asked him about it then.

"Oh, you found something that is concerning to you?" he said calmly. At the same time, however, he seemed to be breathing heavily on the other end of the line. It was as if he was engaged in some kind of sporting activity while talking. "Listen, Grace, I never said you couldn't go up there. I'm sure we can discuss whatever you found. But could it wait until I'm back home?"

Martijn made a strange and sudden kind of outburst on the line that sounded like a grunt—"Ugh!"—as if he was throwing something heavy, like a big suitcase maybe, into a car.

"What are you doing over there?" she asked.

"Oh, just"—he paused, grunting again—"setting up a tent."

He made a series of loud groans on the other end of the line, which gave her the impression that he was digging something, but actually they might even have been sexual noises. "Am I interrupting you?" she asked, trying to keep the sarcasm out of her tone, not sure if she had succeeded.

"Not at all," he said. "But this may not be the best time to talk. We're trying to set up camp. Is there something else?"

Grace couldn't hear any background noise, no sounds of anyone else talking. Who was the "we" he was referring to? If he was with the other Scout leaders, they were probably all separately doing their own thing, apart from one another, in the great outdoors. She pressed the phone closer to her ear.

"And your computer was on and open," she lied. "I was trying to Google something and I ended up opening some photo files. I guess I was just curious what kinds of things you're looking at when you're up there, and..."

"Nothing to be curious about," he said, and she could hear a scold in his voice. Yes, this had been crossing a line. She knew that, even if she was downplaying it. "Any man needs his space, you know. I just need a place where I can sit and smoke a cigar and not be bothered."

Ah, the cigars. Maybe that was all it was, actually. A place where he could go and secretly smoke.

"I didn't even know you were smoking cigars," she said, trying not to sound priggish.

"Well," he said. "A man does need to have a few secrets." He laughed. Then he blurted out, "Ugh, whoo," as if he was moving furniture around.

"What is going on over there? Is it really hard to set up the tents?"

"No, I'm done with that," he said. "Firewood."

Then there was the sound of something heavy falling,

and if Grace could trust her ears, she heard another voice, vaguely in the background. Not someone talking but more like a woman sighing. "Oh," she said. "With the other supervisors, I guess."

Could he be having an affair? Could it be that simple after all? Could it all come down to that?

"Whew," he said, now sounding like he was trying to catch his breath. "Big logs. Grace, listen," he added, speaking rather sternly. "I'll need to call you back. This is a much larger conversation. I'll call you back once we're settled in."

CHAPTER 15

MIDNIGHT RAID

If there was one skill Karin had learned from her father, it was how to, as he put it, "move like a ghost." He said the key to it was to try to stay loose. When your body gets stiff, you're likely to make weird movements that send you off-balance and make you trip. So then you might be able to be quiet for a while and then you suddenly tumble to the ground. He had done this moving like a ghost to blend into the background as a war photographer. Now she needed to do it to make sure she could get away from this ghoul camp.

As the rain was gently pattering on the green tarp that covered them in their makeshift den, and they seemed to be slumbering in their ponchos, right there in the dirt, she decided to make her move. A few hours had probably already passed since they found her by the tree, and the Scouts and her leaders must be wondering where on earth she had gone to. She hoped they might be looking for her already, but she somehow doubted they'd be near here.

It was hard for her to orient herself, but she didn't bother to look for her compass again. If it had still been in her backpack, it was now somewhere in the mud, where they had dumped out her backpack hours ago. They'd taken her tinder kit, mess kit, and of course her knife, and complained that she had only a euro and twenty-five cents of money, and no pills. They'd eaten the candy bars and emergency food supplies she'd brought with her, and left her extra set of dry clothes, including her favorite T-shirt, in a heap in the mud. Ghouls or vampires or whatever, they were definitely creeps.

If it seemed at first like they might help her, it soon became clear that they were wholly uninterested in anything but themselves.

The one who spoke to her the most, the leader with the acrid breath and the translucent skin, after dumping the contents of her backpack on the ground, had announced that she could stay the night but she'd better not expect them to feed her. She had watched as they pried open tin cans filled with something that looked alarmingly like dog food—Karin really hoped it wasn't, but she couldn't read labels in the dark—and hadn't felt the least bit hungry anyway. Eventually, she had thought, she would be back with the Scouts and they would give her hot dogs and fries with mayonnaise. Nothing in the world had seemed more delicious, at that moment, than the thought of that. But first, she'd had to wait a long time for them all to fall asleep.

Karin decided she would just leave her backpack where it was and make a break for it. All her extra clothes had gotten dirty anyway, and they'd eaten all her food. The only thing she thought she wanted was the backpack itself, which her mom had bought for her at the start of secondary school that year. Since it had a zebra print, she thought maybe she could spot it in the dark.

She was half crouching, half standing when there was a

sudden noise behind her and Karin turned. Nothing. Someone had shifted in their sleep maybe? Then she tried to stand up a little more, and she heard the noise again. Was it coming from under the tarp, or outside? Was someone awake in here, or was there something to fear out there?

Karin could feel her chest start to constrict and her breathing get shorter. *Stay loose,* she told herself. *Stay relaxed. Don't trip.* There was the sound again: something rustling, something moving, something...walking. *Oh no...*

Whatever it was, she didn't want to wait to find out. And at any second, because of the noise it was making, the others would wake up and see her standing there, getting ready to go. She had to "be decisive," as her father would say.

In an instant, Karin made up her mind to run. As soon as she did, all hell seemed to break loose. Suddenly there were flashlights everywhere and bodies surrounding the tarp. Not the people who had taken her captive but other people, from outside the camp, wearing different clothes, a flash of something that looked like a shield, and shouting obscenities: "Get the fuck up!" "Move your asses!" "We know what's going on here!"

Karin was already running when she heard the others waking up and screaming in response. Then she was running faster, as fast as her legs could take her. She heard the sound of something popping, like fireworks on New Year's Eve. Could it be guns? Was someone shooting? She didn't wait to find out or look back; she just kept running, leaping, driving through the woods to get as far away from there as possible. She was only a kid! Who would be firing a gun at her?

She whipped through the forest, the wet leaves of the trees smacking into her face, the branches scratching her shoulders and chest, jabbing at her sometimes so she had to fend them off like arrows. She smashed through the foliage, forearms raised in front of her face to guard off more attacks; she nearly got a twig in her eye but managed to bat it out of her face just seconds before it gouged her. Breathing heavily and using every ounce of her energy, she dodged and ducked and kept her legs moving as fast as she could, propelled forward by terror.

At long last, when she felt her breathing becoming too difficult and bile rising in the back of her throat, she stopped. Putting her hands against the trunk of a wide tree, she dropped her head and tried to suck air into her lungs. She could feel her legs trembling underneath her and her knees throbbing. Tears came pouring out of her eyes uncontrollably as she heaved in air—as much as she could swallow. She coughed and spit. Then she listened.

Nothing. No sound of anyone coming after her. No pop-pop firecracker sound in the distance. No sound at all, except the rustle of leaves. She had gotten away. No one had come after her. No one had followed her through the woods. She was alone.

She was alone. And now she had no compass, no back-pack, no clothes, no map, no food, no water, and obviously no phone. Only the clothes on her back, which were wet with sweat and clinging. And she had no clue anymore where she was.

But this time, she told herself, she was not going to cry.

CHAPTER 16

BLOOD

Grace had finished packing Karin's suitcase and was back in her own bedroom. She had finally called a friend, an old friend named Jenny, the one who lived in The Hague and worked at the International Criminal Court there. They'd met each other in pregnancy yoga long, long ago, but they'd maintained a connection, as two Americans living abroad, and checked in with each other every once in a while.

Because of Jenny's work as a prosecutor at the ICC, she had understood the context of Pieter's work. They too had been friends, and she and Pieter had sometimes engaged in long, even heated political discussions over wine or whiskey, way into the night. Grace thought of Jenny as part of her "old life," and Martijn had never met her. Which was another reason why she might be a good person to visit at a time like this—Grace wasn't exactly planning to *run away* from Martijn, but she felt it might be wise to go somewhere he wasn't likely to find her.

"Look, I think there's a very good chance that all of this can be explained simply," said Jenny, echoing her own doubts. "Just discuss it when he's back home. It's hard to talk to someone on a camping trip on a mobile phone. He's in one universe and you're in another."

"I still feel like I need to get out of here and get my head together," said Grace.

"Perfect, then come and visit us. It's been way too long since I've seen you, and a weekend away with Karin should be within the reasonable limits of a healthy marriage," she said. "Just pop down. Once you've had a couple of days to yourself, you'll figure out the right way to discuss this."

Grace was talking while standing on a stepladder trying to reach a felt storage box that contained her father's coin collection, her mother's precious jewelry, and a handful of critical documents they'd need, just in case they never returned to this house: social security cards, notarized documents, mortgage records, that sort of thing...She was probably overreacting, she told herself. But, well...

"Remember when you guys came down a few years ago and we had such a nice time visiting the Binnenhof and the Mauritshuis?" said Jenny. "I'd love to do that again. This very lovely restaurant just opened around the corner that serves oysters on the half shell and very contemporary gin and tonics. Should we do that?"

Jenny was trying to help calm Grace's nerves, when probably they both knew the only thing they'd be able to muster during this emotional crisis was a bottle of whiskey after the kids were in bed. "Oysters," Grace said, as if they were relics from another time and another universe, where there was still anything to celebrate.

The phone started to beep as if another call was coming through. "It must be Martijn," she told Jenny. "I should take that."

"Of course you should," said Jenny. "Try to keep it . . . chill."

"Yes," said Grace. "Chill."

No matter what Martijn had to say this time, Grace planned to do exactly what Jenny had laid out for her: She'd put a couple of bags into the trunk of the car. When Karin's dropping was over, she'd pick up her daughter, and they'd drive down to The Hague. The tricky part was to try to figure out what to say to Martijn, since he didn't always like it when she made plans to see her friends without him. If she played it off all casual, it probably would be okay. He didn't know Jenny, so he didn't need to see her too, right?

She answered the line that was ringing, "Hello, honey," doing her best to sound chipper and completely unagitated.

Suddenly there was a deluge of Dutch words coming at her, an unfamiliar voice, high-pitched and somewhat disconcerting.

"I'm sorry, can you speak a little bit slower?" Grace answered in Dutch. "I can't really understand what you're saying." Although Grace spoke Dutch, she sometimes couldn't entirely follow if a person spoke quickly or with an unfamiliar accent.

"English?" said the caller. "Are you English?"

"I'm American," she said. "But I speak Dutch, if you wouldn't mind speaking a bit slower."

"Are. You. Karin?" the caller asked, staying in English, and trying to slow down and speak clearly so Grace would be able to follow.

"I'm not Karin; I'm her mother," said Grace. "I'm Karin's mother," she repeated, not hearing anything on the line. "Is something the matter?"

"We found a girl's T-shirt in the Veluwe," said the caller.

"This phone number was written into the name place on the inside. We thought we would just check if Karin knew it was missing."

Karin was missing her shirt? Surely not the one she had been wearing. Her home phone number had been typed onto little tags they'd sewn into all of Karin's clothes, as part of the preparation for the dropping. The Scouts didn't appreciate lost articles and didn't want the kids to get their clothes confused.

"You are her mother?" said the woman.

"Yes, I'm the mother. Karin is my daughter," she said. "It must have dropped out of her bag, I guess. She's on a camping trip. Where did you find it?"

"I don't call to alarm you," said the woman, slowly and carefully. "Everything is okay. But you are the mother."

Grace found this string of sentences confusing. Nobody says they don't want to alarm you unless you're about to be alarmed.

"The shirt has..." The woman hesitated, before continuing. "The shirt has blood on it."

"I'm sorry, what? Blood?" Grace swallowed. "Is Karin hurt?"

"No," said the woman. "I don't know where Karin is. That's why I'm calling. We found the shirt in *de bos*. In the forest. Karin wasn't with it."

Grace felt her mouth get suddenly very dry. "Where's Karin, then? And what do you mean, that her shirt has blood on it?" She knew already that this woman didn't have these answers, but the questions had spilled out of her mouth anyway.

The woman on the other end of the line seemed to understand that she had indeed stirred up confusion. She slowed down and spoke more calmly. "Can we speak Dutch?" she asked. "It's easier for me."

Grace agreed, and the rest of the conversation took place in Dutch.

"Listen, I really don't mean to upset you. I will assume it really is nothing," she said. "I'm a mother too, and I would certainly be concerned if I got this phone call from a stranger. Normally I wouldn't have thought anything of it. Probably it's just a lost piece of clothing; maybe she dropped it. But I am just that kind of person who likes to dot all the *i*'s and cross all the *t*'s, and I always return a transit card to its owner if I find it—that sort of thing. With just a little bit of extra vigilance, I thought I should call."

"Well, I'm certainly grateful there are people like you in the world," said Grace. She understood that the woman was trying to minimize the fear. But that only served to make her think there was reason to be afraid.

"But Karin is with you, isn't she? She's okay, right?" the woman said.

"No, she's not with me," said Grace, feeling her throat constrict, finding it hard to answer. "She's...she's on a camping trip in the Hoge Veluwe. A dropping. She should be there, with her group, with her Scout leaders. My husband is with her...I'm sorry." She stopped. "Who is this?"

She realized that she was gripping the phone with two hands, holding hard as if it was somehow a way to get a grip on everything.

"I'm, oh, I'm nobody," said the woman. "I was just out walking my dogs. We live near the park and I let them run out there in the evenings. Jezebel is a German shorthair, bred for hunting. We don't hunt, but she's a pretty dog. She sometimes comes back with rabbits or voles between her teeth. It's not pretty, but it's what is in her nature."

She went on, maybe out of nervousness: "This time she came back with this T-shirt in her teeth, and I noticed blood in her mouth. I thought she had killed something. I was confused. Then, you know, I thought maybe her mouth was bleeding. It was very strange. I don't know if I'm doing the right thing. I don't want to worry you. I was just concerned..." She was speaking rapidly, and then finally answered the question. "My name is Maaike. Maaike Bol."

"Thank you, Maaike," said Grace. "Is it possible that the dog attacked something and then somehow found the T-shirt after that?"

"Oh yes, anything is possible," said the woman. "I don't know. I'm not a forensic scientist or anything like that. I have no way of knowing. But I just... If you don't mind my asking, how old is Karin?"

Grace's mind had gone off in a million directions, with just as many questions. She was already making a list in her head of all the people she needed to call. "Please hold on to the shirt, just as it is. Don't wash it or anything. I am going to make a few calls to the people who are supervising Karin, and if they are with her, I will agree it's nothing. If not, you'll be hearing back from me shortly."

"How old is Karin?" Maaike Bol repeated.

"She's... she's twelve," Grace said. "I'm sorry, but I need to hang up so I can check on her now. I have your number. I'll call you back."

CHAPTER 17

WILD THINGS

I've made it through the woods, Karin thought. She tried to muster up a sense of pride in her journey so far, but she was still so creeped out and kind of trembling. Everything that had happened in the last hours was so messed up. What even *was* that? Who were those freaky people, and could that really have been a *gunshot* she heard when she ran away? She'd never heard a gunshot in her life. Only in movies and on TV.

All she knew was, it was good that she had gotten away, and she was safe. She was okay.

It had to be after midnight, like, probably *way* after midnight by now. The air had turned much colder, and she was all wet and shivering. It didn't feel good at all, but she told herself, *I'm not going to die. It's just sweat,* as her father would have.

As she stepped into an open space, she saw more of the weird twisted dead trees, which she knew so well. They didn't bother her now. Past that, she saw an upright block of wood that had markings on it. Arrows and numbers. It was a trail! A well-worn path, a pale yellowish path of sand and dirt, which almost glowed white in the moonlight. She didn't have a map that would've told her which trail this was, so the markings didn't make much sense. Was it the trail that would lead to the campsite? She didn't care about cocoa and hot dogs, but she wanted to find the grown-ups she was supposed to find. She needed to find them to get back to her mom.

She felt nearly giddy as she looked up and could see stars between what was left of the clouds. If things hadn't gotten all messed up, they would all be sitting around the campfire right now, leaning back and staring up at the sky and counting those stars. Or picking out constellations with their Scout guides. Or else they'd just be talking, like regular people do, about nothing at all, and having fun. That's what she should have been doing. She felt a lump in her throat, imagining all that she was missing. The other kids had to be there already and she was the only one who was lost. Were they thinking about her? Would someone come out to try to find her?

Karin knew things didn't go the way they were supposed to go pretty much ever. Case in point: people's fathers weren't supposed to die all of a sudden. Especially when their daughters were ten. Moms weren't supposed to fall to pieces. People weren't supposed to ask if it was her father's fault that he got killed, or suggest that he'd been doing something he wasn't supposed to be doing over there, especially when he was working for all of us—to inform all of us about what was happening in parts of the world nobody wanted to know about. Moms weren't supposed to remarry that fast, and not to their father's boss or his accountant or whatever he was.

Kids at school weren't supposed to treat you bad because your dad was killed. They weren't supposed to just stare at you from afar and act like you had some contagious disease. People you didn't even know weren't supposed to all of a sudden pretend to be your friends, like school counselors and teachers and everyone above the age of ten. Strangers weren't supposed to call your house at random. Stepdads weren't supposed to get so strange so fast, were they? And say creepy things to you and follow you to school? Moms were supposed to notice these things, weren't they? They were supposed to protect you.

Karin was on her own now, out here, in the night, in the big, giant national park, which wasn't supposed to be scary at all. Nothing, everyone said, was really dangerous in the Netherlands. It was so safe here. Maybe it was on the outside. Maybe it was for other people. But for Karin? Not really.

That was part of the reason she had joined Scouts, to get out here and to do the dropping this summer. She wanted to get away and be able to take care of herself. She wanted to be away from home for a while. To not hear the screaming and fighting and noise of Martijn hurting her mother downstairs. To get away from him—that weird way he had of watching her all the time. Not like he came into her room or anything, but he kind of hovered. It wasn't normal.

But then the a-hole had volunteered to be the parent guide on this trip. What a creep. Why couldn't he let her just go away for a weekend? It was like he somehow had to own her and her mom. Her mom had once told her that it was "good to have a man around the house, to keep us safe." Ha. What kind of dumb thing was that? They were *way* safer without him.

Karin realized that she had been walking looking down at her feet, so she decided to look up and not think so hard, because thinking hard sometimes started to feel really bad.

She saw shapes in front of her—a big, wide tree next to a pair of large boulders—and all of a sudden, something started to make sense. Those shapes were familiar. She knew where she was. She recognized those shapes, even in the darkness. She had been here before. She'd spent a lot of time next to those two boulders.

Could it be? Were her eyes tricking her? Or was it just déjà vu? Her mom had said that was just some tickling in your brain that made you think you recognized something you didn't.

No, those two boulders and that tree were totally familiar. She *had* been here before. With her dad. This was their place! The mouflon place! They'd come here a lot of times to photograph the most beautiful creatures in the park, the mouflons. Karin loved them the most. They were like sheep, or goats, but they had these crazy long horns that wrapped around in huge arcs, like long Princess Leia hair buns. They had white noses and white feet, and the rest of their bodies were brown. She and her dad had come here every year for a few years to shoot pictures of them in springtime, when there were new babies—they were called ewes and lambs.

Somewhere right here was...yes, over there, the bridge across that little stream, made from pine branches. It was the same. Even just in the moonlight, she recognized it. They always pitched their tent just near that leaning tree there. This was the place where they'd also had their last Veluwe camping trip together, just before Dad went back to Syria for the last time. Just before he was killed. This place was the reason she'd wanted to come back to the Veluwe.

She stopped and caught her breath. She knew where she

was! Incredible! Glorious. She wasn't lost, actually. Not that she was where she was supposed to be. But she was here. She was actually where she had wanted to be.

At almost exactly that same moment, and before she could truly celebrate, she heard a sound that made her shudder. It wasn't close, because it was kind of soft, but it was definitely a sound she recognized: the howl of a wolf. It sounded like a creaky door opening, only very loud.

Oh geez, thought Karin. *Can I really not catch a break?*

It was almost, *almost* funny. Her mom had been reading her those articles all spring and summer, and Karin had been telling her there was literally no reason to worry. "It's a huge forest," Karin had said. "How likely is it that *our* group is going to bump into them?"

But now she wasn't part of a group and now she could hear them. Not super near—but that was definitely the sound of a wolf, or at least one of them, howling. And that was pretty scary by itself.

The wolf howled again. It didn't sound the way it sounded in movies, not so sharp and not so distinct, like "Awoohoo." More like a series of dog barks and then a baby crying from a bad stomachache. Then came another howl, and then after that a second, a little bit softer, which had to be a reply. Which meant there were at least two wolves out there. Talking.

Karin felt a kind of fist clench in the pit of her stomach. She had no supplies at all now. Not a knife or a flashlight. Not even a spoon. What could she use to protect herself if somehow she actually bumped into the wolf her mother had been tracking all summer? She remembered Lotte's words from hours ago—now it seemed like years ago: "So there's a wolf *pack* out here?" Seven, she knew. Her mother knew.

She searched the ground around her, looking for a stick. At the very least, she could fend them off with a stick. Karin tried to remember what her mother had taught her about wolf encounters. Don't turn you back on them and run away. Either move forward, flapping your hands, and yell at them, or walk slowly backward, also yelling. Yelling was important, because wolves were normally afraid of people. It wasn't easy to find a good stick because everything around her was brush, heath. And anyway, what was she going to do—poke it in the eye?

There. There was one. It was about as long as her arm, and she could just swing it around, if necessary. That would work. She held it out in front of her as she walked. The howls came again, and this time they sounded closer, but she thought: *They aren't that close. That's just my mind playing tricks on me.* And then, with her fear getting the better of her, she really picked up her pace.

Karin tried to remember something else, to distract herself from the howling—which continued, like a song, call and response, call and response. More than one. More than a few. Her father. Their last trip here. Being with him in this forest.

The thing that popped into her head was that he had stopped off at the grocery store on the way to the park that night and bought a six-pack of those tall beers. She remembered it because those cans made so much noise when you opened them—the pop and then the hiss—which obviously was not good for watching wildlife. He had always been so careful about that. Before, when he did drink, it was something like scotch, out of a flask, but usually only on a cold night.

After he died, people said that he maybe had been careless

in Syria. People on the news sounded like there was some chance he'd kind of brought the sniper attack on himself. People said such annoying things! Then the things they said got in your head and it was hard to get them out. People had said that her dad was a drunk, and that was totally not true. Her mom had told her to try to ignore all the rumors, "all that media nonsense," and not even watch the news reports about her father's death because all kinds of untrue things got said.

"But why did Daddy get killed?" Karin had asked at the time, but she was younger then. Mom had told her, "Sweetheart, people get killed in wars. Hundreds of thousands of people have died there. Almost half a million. Your father was just one of them. He was unlucky, but it was not his fault." The most important thing for the two of them to do, her mom had said, was to remember her father the way he had been when they knew him, and to try to hold on to all the good things he had brought to their lives. And that was how Karin wanted to think about him. But it was annoying how many different things there were now in her head. People could really mess with your brain.

Like Martijn. When they were alone, when Mom wasn't there, he would say such strange things about her father. Like things that didn't make any sense. Like that he was a risk-taker. And that he was an "adventurer," and the way he said those things didn't sound like he meant them as compliments. And when Karin asked him how Martijn could know anything about her father, he claimed that he "knew him pretty well." She didn't even know what that was supposed to mean. Martijn didn't know her father. She knew her father. Her mom knew her father. Martijn was nobody to them.

Then Martijn would ask her all kinds of questions about her father that she couldn't answer. And even if she could answer, why would she tell *him*? Maybe her mom trusted him, but that didn't mean she had to. She didn't have to. He wasn't her dad. She didn't even want him to be her stepdad, but her mom kept telling her it would be better for them. That was so totally untrue.

Karin remembered only her father's best parts most of the time—except sometimes when she let a little bit of the rest of it seep through, get into her brain, make her confused. Why did the whole world think they could say anything they wanted to about him now? Why didn't they realize that he had been her dad and that meant something?

The weekend when they camped here, Karin remembered, she had just unzipped the door to their tent when the mouflons came onto that hillside. First she saw one ewe and then another, and her breath caught. She held it and inched slowly back into the tent to wake her father, who was still asleep. "They're here," she said softly. "They're just outside." He propped himself up on his elbows inside his sleeping bag, suddenly alert. "Get your camera," she whispered.

He reached over and pulled his camera bag toward him, then spun around with the whole sleeping bag, without getting out of it. Then he walked on his elbows toward the opening of the tent, and the two of them peered out together. It was a foggy morning, and a soft light shimmered through the mist that hovered over the damp ground.

The mouflons came, one after another, and then another and another until there were at least two dozen of them, and then four dozen of them, and then nearly—it must have been—a hundred. They were standing on the hill and looking out over the landscape, like, just checking out the view. How gentle they were, and how peaceful. And this was their park, their home. It certainly didn't belong to Karin and her father. For them to be okay out here, they needed supplies, sleeping bags and tents and food and equipment. They were trespassers. The mouflons, these wild sheep with their strange, helmet-like ram horns, were the owners.

After he took the pictures, her father just went back to sleep, which was odd. Normally he was a real early riser and loved to get out and go hiking for the whole morning, before lunch. Karin got up and went for a walk, gathering kindling. No one passed by, and the mouflons were gone.

Feeling bored being all alone, she came back to the campsite. She found him still sleeping. So she decided to wake him up. When she whispered in his ear, "Dad...Dad? It's time to get up," he swatted at her like she was a mosquito buzzing around him. It was very strange—very unlike him.

Finally, he rolled over and looked at her, his eyes bloodshot and his hair wild, as if he was waking from a manic dream. "Sweetheart, it's you," he said, like he was surprised she was on the trip with him. "What time is it?"

She told him that it was already after 11 a.m. "Is it?" he said, bolting up. "Oh wow. I was really out of it. I had no idea that it was already that late. I'm sorry."

He was still in his sleeping bag, and he looked like he'd taken a bath in there. His shirt was soaked. Karin said he didn't have to say sorry. But she wondered if maybe he was sick or something.

He got up and got dressed, and they ate cold muesli next to the dead embers of the fire from the night before. He didn't bother making a new fire with the kindling she'd collected, as they sometimes did in the early morning to cook oatmeal and brew hot coffee and warm milk. Her father just said, "Let's go to the museum," where he could buy some coffee, forgetting about their plan to go hiking. He just wasn't in the mood to work anymore, he said; he had too much on his mind.

They'd packed up the whole camping trip and biked to the museum. Karin remembered that they had seen Vincent van Gogh's paintings, lots of dark images of awkwardly shaped figures with kind of bulgy eyes sitting in dreary rooms in tiny houses or working huge looms. She liked the ones of people in the fields, holding big sacks of whatever it was they were picking. Her favorite, though, was a picture of a yellow café with lots of chairs outside, under a blue sky filled with stars. She'd asked her father if he would buy her the poster, and he did. She'd hung it up in her bedroom but took it down after he died.

Wait a minute, thought Karin, stopping in her tracks. *If this is where we were camping, then the museum is not so far away.* If she had a bike, she could get there in maybe fifteen minutes. Walking, it would take longer, of course, but it was that way—toward that large cluster of pine trees. She was sure of that.

But if she got there now, it would be closed. It was the middle of the night. Did it make sense to go there and just wait there until morning? Or maybe she should go and find a security guard or something.

Still, if the museum was straight ahead, then that direction was north, and the Otterlose Forest was to the west, or left. If she was where she thought she was, then she wasn't so far from the Scouts' campsite either. It had to be within a half-hour walk, then. Maybe she should just go there. The Scout leaders would certainly still be at the campsite, waiting for her. Now she finally had a sense of direction. For the first time in hours she felt hopeful that she would actually make it there!

Feeling a bit better, she chugged up a little hill and rounded a curve in the trail. She was about to start running down the hill but stopped short. There, right in front of her, were two bright shining eyes. Yellow eyes. She could see them even in the dark. Then she made out the golden fur around its chin and its ears, standing upright. It was a wolf.

CHAPTER 18

HERE AND GONE

Grace fumbled to find the button to press to end the call, and realized as soon as she'd done it that she could not call Karin because Karin had deposited her telephone into a black velvet sack that was now in the possession of the Scout leader in charge of the trip. What was her name? Grace was sure she could not remember. They'd only met for the first time that morning, because there had been a swapping of Scout leaders, for some reason, at the last minute. Someone had gotten sick…it didn't matter why. What was her name?

Well, the obvious person to call was Martijn. If she called him again, he'd probably think she was somehow just going mad while he was out there quietly trying to enjoy nature. Talk about violating his need for "space." But of course these kinds of moments had to override all that domain building, didn't it? He was her partner, her husband; he had to be concerned about Karin's welfare first.

It was ridiculous that she was even debating this with herself. When had she become such a second-guesser of her own will and needs? She pressed his number and waited for him to answer. She'd of course explain it and he'd of course feel as concerned as she did.

But he did not pick up the phone this time. It rang and rang, and finally she heard his message: *"Ik ben er helaas niet. Laat een bericht achter de..."* She hung up.

Martijn often went incommunicado. It didn't have to be because of a fight. Sometimes something she said would irk him, and then, without warning, he'd just disappear. There was a piano bar called De Nachtwacht, where they sang Dutch ballads far too loudly, and sometimes he'd end up there. It was a harmless activity, basically, and it was a good way to shake off some tension, she reasoned. The bartender would call her if he'd had one too many, to bring him home. He was almost reliably there, unless he wasn't.

Grace would try not to ask where he'd been when he came back, because asking that just meant she was as controlling as he always accused her of being. It was true that she had a possessive side, but was hers so much more drastic, as he would have it, than that of anyone else who loved someone? But, she'd wondered so many times, was this love? Did he love her if he was always feeling this angry at her, always in either fight or flight? Was she actually that hard to take? Was it love if he didn't pick up his phone?

Panicking a bit now, Grace remembered that she had been given a list of emergency phone contact numbers this morning from the new Scout leader of the trip. What was her name? It was on a piece of paper she'd folded up and put somewhere. In a pocket or a purse. But what purse had she taken this morning?

Paper! It was maddening. Who used paper anything anymore? She was not going to waste valuable time looking for a piece of paper. She must know one of these people's numbers. The man who had driven them, she thought. Grace could remember his name; she'd met him before, somewhere, at a hockey parent gathering. Something like that. He was somebody's father. But her mind was completely blank. She should not lose her wits now. She had to hold it together.

Grace forced herself to slow down. She held on to the back of a chair, dropped her head, and took a series of deep breaths. Breathing. She had to do it—yoga and meditation had in fact taught her a few useful things. If she slowed her breathing, she could slow down the world, just a little bit, stop its turning.

Rutger—yes, Rutger. The driver's name had been Rutger. Breathing was good.

But as she scrolled through her contacts on her smartphone, she could see that her hand was trembling nonetheless. She heard her own breaths, shorter and tighter again. Finally she found the number for Rutger and punched it in to make the call. But it didn't work, probably because her index finger had jabbed at the phone too quickly. She hung up and tried again.

Once she had gotten the number right, he picked up immediately. "Hello, you're speaking with Rutger," he said, rather formally, in Dutch.

"Rutger," she said. "Thank God you answered. It's Grace, Karin's mom. I just had the strangest call. Please tell me that Karin is there with all of you, safe and sound."

"Oh, Grace," he started. "Is there something the matter?"

"Is Karin there? Did she make it to the camp yet?"

There was an excruciatingly long pause, during which Grace wished she could put her hand through the phone and grab Rutger and shake him.

"She hasn't gotten here yet, no not yet," he said grimly. "The kids haven't made it to the site yet. They are still finding their way."

"Is that...?" Grace just wanted to come out and ask for reassurances. "Is that normal? That must be normal, right?"

Rutger paused again. "It really depends on the group. Sometimes it can take longer and sometimes it is shorter." There was a dry and officious way he was answering all the questions that Grace found irksome, but this was what people liked to refer to as "typical Dutch." Noncommittal and middle of the road. In her mind, a useless answer.

"Could I—" Grace started. "Would you mind putting my husband on the phone? I tried his cell, but he didn't pick up. I'm sure he must be tending to the fire or something, and I don't want to interrupt your activities, but it's important. Something has come up."

Grace couldn't tell if Rutger's next long pause was the result of a poor connection, a problem with finding the right officious answer, or some actual dementia on his part, but she was about to scream when he finally said, "Oh, Martijn isn't here at the campsite. He went as the backup leader. Meaning, he went behind the kids. Riekje and I came ahead to set up the camp, and Riekje just left to track back and be the front guide. I'm staying at the campsite to welcome them when they arrive, preparing the sausages and hot chocolate."

This new information did not correlate with what she thought she already knew about Martijn's whereabouts. She'd heard him setting up the camp with the others, hadn't she? "But I spoke to him earlier tonight, and he said he was setting up the campsite, hauling logs, with you."

Rutger laughed, a sign of human life. "Ha ha, no, we aren't doing any hauling of logs over here. They send us out with precut timber. The park has rules about using local wood. Not allowed. Makes it easier, and more environmentally sustainable. When they came in, Martijn chose to follow the group, and Riekje and I came here." His tone in the last part suggested that he might be irritated at having to repeat himself because she somehow failed to grasp the protocol.

Grace wasn't going to start to question what a "backup leader" was supposed to do. But she gathered that Martijn was following the group, probably not far behind, to make sure they were safely making their way. That was what she had been told when they signed up for the dropping—that the kids would certainly feel like they were on their own in the woods, but in fact there would be plenty of adult supervision. The adults would be just a little bit ahead and a little bit behind, and if the kids got lost, there was a pretty vast safety net. The important thing was that they had the sense they had to make their own way out there. But they didn't, really.

Now she was miffed. Why was it that at every turn she had the feeling she couldn't trust her eyes and ears, or what Martijn was telling her? A piece of information she'd received conflicted directly with her own impression of things. Was this something Martijn was doing? There was a word for this, if this was what this was: "gaslighting." A term she'd always liked, because it came from that wonderful black-and-white movie with a young, stunning Ingrid Bergman. She is married to a man who is trying to steal her inheritance; he seems to have his wife's best interests at heart, but in the night he's trying to rob her, up in the attic.

When he goes up there to search for jewels, she notices the lights dim, because the gas powering the lights in the house is being diverted to light that extra room. But he tells her that can't be happening—something that doesn't jibe with what can be directly observed. She begins to not trust herself, thinking she's going mad.

Could Martijn be doing something like this to her? Or was she, perhaps, actually just going mad, like he sometimes accused?

Grace waited to try to collect her thoughts. Certain things were clearly true. "Some lady just called me and said that she found Karin's T-shirt in the forest," said Grace. "And she told me the T-shirt may have blood on it."

"What?" This time Rutger's response was at lightning speed. "Wait, what?"

She repeated herself. "Karin's T-shirt was found by someone, some stranger in the Veluwe. She said it was bloody. I don't know why that would be. Do you have any idea why that would be?"

There was silence on the other end of the phone, but Grace understood that this time it was a stunned silence. "I...I don't know what that means," he said when he finally spoke. "I do not understand that. She was with the group when we last saw her. I have no reason to believe that anything has gone wrong, or that anyone lost anything. They haven't arrived at the campsite yet, but that seems normal. We were here, setting up, waiting for them. Your husband followed them, and Riekje is on her way to guide them here. Nobody's hurt, as far as I know. I'll call around. But I'd recommend you contact your husband. He's the one who's currently most directly in charge of the group."

Somehow this last statement sent a chill up Grace's spine.

But as soon as she felt it, she told herself that her feeling was wrong, absurd. Martijn wouldn't hurt children. He certainly wouldn't hurt Karin. What had gotten into her? She'd somehow spooked herself about her own husband. None of that was happening.

Still, it would be pitch-black out there in the forest, she thought. Even if the kids were together, how would they handle some kind of situation that involved blood?

"I couldn't reach Martijn," Grace said. "I sincerely hope Riekje finds them. Will you call her?"

"Yes, I'll do that right now. Who was the woman who called you? Did she say who she was?" asked Rutger, who was clearly trying to offer Grace moral support. But she didn't want to stay on the phone anymore. She needed some other course of action.

"A complete stranger," Grace said, but now she was getting antsy. She had to get off the phone.

"Try Martijn again," said Rutger. "He was just behind them on the trail. Maybe he's already caught up with them. It's possible someone fell down and got a cut and they used an extra T-shirt because they didn't have a Band-Aid. Something like that. I'm sure it's something that simple. Martijn would be in the best position to know."

A pang of terror traveled down her spine this time. But why? Okay, it was strange that he had those documents and files from Pieter, but what on earth would that have to do with this dropping? Martijn wasn't a violent man, generally speaking. As far as she knew, he had only ever physically hurt one person, and that was her, Grace.

"Yes, it's a good idea to call him," she answered perfunctorily. "There's probably some perfectly reasonable explanation for this." She should start to count the number

131

of times she'd tried to assuage her own fears using the same exact phrase just today. "I'll call you back if I find out anything."

She hung up and leaned over, propping her elbows on her knees, feeling like she might vomit. Taking about four deep breaths in and out, she tried to prepare herself for what would come next. Then she swiped open her phone again and speed-dialed Martijn. She heard it ring and clutched the phone close to her ear, saying, "Come on, come on, pick up, pick up, asshole." She was absolutely sure he would pick up this time. He had to. He had to provide some explanation. But it rang and rang and rang.

Grace grabbed the two suitcases she had already packed and carried them down the stairs. Her plan was starting now. She was going to find this woman, she was going to the forest, and then she was going to find Karin in the Veluwe herself. And then they were going to The Hague, to Jenny, and they were not coming back here. Not until everything, and that meant every single thing, was somehow straight in her head.

She redialed the woman. "Hello, it's me, Karin's mother, Grace. I'd like to come and get the T-shirt, see it. Maybe it will help me figure out what's going on. Where do you live?"

The woman seemed to have been waiting by the phone for her return call. She told Grace her address and said she'd be there when she arrived. "I know this is not possible," she added. "But try not to worry. I'm sure your daughter is all right. It's probably just a false alarm."

Grace thanked her and hung up, throwing the suitcases into the trunk and getting into the car. She needed to be there now. She needed to fly there. Not another second could be wasted. She needed to have her daughter in her arms.

CHAPTER 19

PACK OF WOLVES

No, it was not just one wolf. It was the whole family. The big one was up in front, and its eyes were glinting at her. Was that the mom or the dad? She could see the outlines of the little ones behind, one after another stepping out from the brush, like they were a gang assembling for a street fight. They didn't look really mean or anything, but Karin was freaked.

Karin froze. The big one stood there, just staring at her. And Karin stood there, staring at him...or her. If it was the mom, then that could be worse, because the mom would be really protective of her young and she might need to attack Karin. If it was the dad, well, maybe the same. Karin didn't know. The wolf barked like a dog for a second and gave a really, really big howl. Loud and piercing, like it wanted to send an alarm.

Holy, holy crap. Karin probably would have run away— in spite of her mom's advice—if only she could move a single muscle. But her body was just not doing anything. It was like she was stuck in stone. Her arms were, like, paralyzed, and because of that she had dropped her stick on the ground. No way was she bending down to pick it up.

No way would she have waved it around anyway. Her arms were not moving. Her feet were stuck in concrete, and her legs started to tremble. She could not run, no way.

For a moment that seemed like an eternity, nothing at all happened. They were like two school enemies, finding themselves alone on a playground, just standing there, sussing each other out. Who would make the first move?

He wasn't a black wolf, like she'd seen in movies. He was more grayish and golden, kind of like a big version of a red fox. In the app they used to track his movements, her mom had shown her pictures of him. She'd seen him in a lot of nighttime photos—those infrared photos hunters sometimes took at night—black and white, with his eyes looking like two demonic white dots. This was *the* Veluwe wolf, or maybe his mate, but she didn't see another adult wolf. She saw only a couple of the cubs, but the others had to be near here somewhere. They always traveled in their pack. If she wasn't so scared right now, she might feel honored. He was famous.

Time was ticking by. Moments. Something was going to happen if she just kept standing there. She had to do something. If she tried to run, she knew the wolf would attack. She had to either start slowly backing away—which would make her seem weak and maybe vulnerable—or she had to somehow muster up the courage to start yelling at him and waving her hands like her mom had told her.

But still, she was frozen.

It felt like one of those nightmares where you only have to call for help, and you open your mouth, but nothing comes out. You try to scream, but your voice has disappeared. It felt like that for about ten seconds, but then the wolf started to move toward her. Two steps and then three steps and then four...Then she saw the other sets of eyes, the rest of the cubs, creeping up behind him.

Karin forced it out. She started to yell and scream bloody murder. She started at a high pitch but then got into the deepest, meanest, manliest voice she could find: "Get out of here, get away from me, you beast! Go away! Go away, leave me alone, don't come near me!" She was suddenly flapping her hands and making a big commotion and even kind of lunging forward and shouting down at him.

At first, he took a few steps back and cocked his head to one side as if trying to figure out if she was some kind of crazy girl. But then she repeated the whole thing over again: "Go away, beast!" shouting even louder and even harder. "Get out! Get out, you nasty beast, get out!" And then he turned toward his own tail and fled. All the little cubs followed him, jumping over rocks and running off through the heath.

And then Karin saw her—it must have been her—the mom, taking up the final position in the pack. To Karin's surprise, she came toward Karin, as if to get a look at this weird figure scaring off her mate, and looked at her. She was curious. She wasn't attacking. She just looked. And then Karin stomped forward, as if she were going to try to grab the mama wolf, and off she fled, following her family, into the dark.

It was a miracle. They were gone. She had scared off a pack of wolves. *Holy crap!*

Karin remained standing where she was until the wolves were clearly out of sight. Then she started to feel her legs tremble violently. The last few minutes—how long could it have been really?—had seemed like they were set to slo-mo, and now it was like a switch had been flipped and she was back in normal time. She started to realize what had just happened. She'd chased off a *pack of wolves* in the forest in the night. It really had been a pack of wolves. She'd done that! And she was only twelve. *Whoa.*

When it hit her like that, Karin's legs just kind of gave way, and she plopped down onto the ground like a rag doll. That was crazy; that had been crazy. And probably no one would ever believe her if she told them what had happened. She didn't have her phone with her, so she couldn't have taken any pictures for evidence. She'd just have to tell people, and then they'd think she was making it up or bragging or something. But it was *true.*

Her legs were still shaking and she was tired, and she was cold and she was alone and she was far from the camp, but she smiled to herself just a little. She was proud of herself for that.

She used her hands to kind of massage her thighs to get them to stop trembling and start working again. When rubbing didn't work, she kind of slammed on them with her fists. They started to tingle and relax, and soon enough she thought she might be able to stand again. It was really weird what fear could do to your body, she thought. How it could make you seize up or freeze or run or leap.

After all she'd been through today already, in less than even twenty-four hours, Karin wondered if she would ever actually be afraid of anything again. She felt like she'd seen it all now. She was kind of a pro at getting out of hairy situations. She was kind of a rock star.

Feeling this new sense of pride, Karin stood up and brushed off her pants. She had a renewed sense that she would make it out of this. There was just one final hurdle, one last leg of her journey. She just had to make it a little bit farther; she just had to walk to the campsite.

Her feet were okay now; her legs worked fine. She didn't even really feel cold anymore because her clothes seemed to be dry—maybe she'd fired up some kind of engine in her body when she was scared and that had warmed everything up. Who knows? There was a hill up ahead, and she climbed it, and when she came down the other side she saw there was another marking on the trail. It felt like the right direction. It must be.

Somewhere along the way, where the path sloped downward into what was sort of a hollow between banks of dirt, she heard what sounded like a human voice, shouting.

It was late and she was tired, and she took it, at first, to be her mind turning the sound of the wind into something else. But then it came again, like a *hoot-hoot*. And when she stopped and listened more carefully, she could make out the words: "Wait!" someone was shouting. "Wait!"

She stopped and turned around, squinting to try to see something on the trail behind her. Nothing there. Convinced again that it was her mind playing tricks on her, she continued hiking, this time walking a little faster than before.

"Up here," she heard, and this time the voice was as clear as a bell. She hadn't been imagining it. "Karin!" came the shout. She looked up, toward the top of the sandy embankment to her left. There, looming over her, was the figure of a man.

"Don't be afraid, Karin," said the voice, which she now realized belonged to her stepfather. "It's just me, Martijn. Wait right there. I'm coming down to get you."

CHAPTER 20

PERFECTLY REASONABLE EXPLANATIONS

Grace had driven this route so many times, with extreme leisure, while listening to a podcast or one of her favorite Stevie Wonder albums, cracking open the window for a bit of fresh air and just coasting.

But this time she sat upright on the edge of her seat, with nothing on but the GPS man, entirely focused on the road, and no distractions, to get there as quickly as possible. The highway stretched out in front of her like an Alfred Hitchcock circle that twisted into infinity. It was so close, and yet it seemed like she would never get there. No matter how hard she stepped on the gas pedal or how much her mind willed her to get there faster, it would still take as much time as it would take.

She was way past the speed limit and aware that if she got too out of control she'd risk getting stopped for a ticket—time she definitely couldn't spare at all. Every second was space, the space between herself and Karin. How would Grace be able to find her now, in the dark, in the sprawling Veluwe, without a phone?

Grace had done her best to convince herself that nothing

was the matter, that there must be some "perfectly reasonable explanation" for the fact that Karin's T-shirt had blood on it, that it was found in the woods, and that the Scout leaders on her trip had not seen her. And a perfectly reasonable explanation for Martijn's refusal to pick up the phone, even though she had tried calling him now at least a dozen times. And a perfectly reasonable explanation for why he had those photos and why he had that file and why he had been behaving aggressively toward her and why their marriage seemed to be built on a foundation of confusion and lies.

The perfectly reasonable explanation completely eluded her—that's what it was. These things might not all be connected, but then again they might. And the perfectly reasonable explanation might encompass all of them at once. Or it might not. Truth be told, the perfectly reasonable explanation might just be that she was going mad. That all of these factors tying her stomach up in knots and making her head feel like it was about to burst a blood vessel were figments of her imagination and signs of her highly troubled mind.

If that was the case, she was okay with it. In fact, that would be good news. Because that would just mean that she would be diagnosed with something and she would get the help she needed, and that everything else in the world was all right. That Karin, most of all, was all right.

As she drove, she kept dialing him again and again, glancing over at the phone briefly and trying not to crash the car in the process. It just rang and rang and rang and rang. *Why??* How idiotic it had been, how utterly stupid of her, to let Martijn go as a supervisor today, of all days, instead of just going herself. She'd wanted to trust him—she'd tried to trust him, beyond how much she actually trusted him—and that was why. But she needed to trust herself. She needed to trust only what she could trust.

As she pressed the gas pedal to the floor, trying to rev the engine of her stupid, ancient urban secondhand sedan, she wondered if the answer to all of her questions was just that: that she'd gone mad. What kind of madness was it? Was it schizophrenia, manic depression? Could it be post-traumatic stress disorder? She had experienced trauma. Or was it generalized anxiety—that was a thing, wasn't it?

The car's GPS man was informing her in his polite British accent that she was supposed to get off the express-way here.

"In two hundred meters, merge into the right lane and take the next exit," he said. Grace was doing her best to be compliant and follow orders, but she knew this wasn't the right exit. She steamed on straight ahead. The voice inter-jected a few moments later, "In eighty meters, turn right. In fifty meters, turn right." The Brit became increasingly insistent—"Turn right here. Turn right here"—but Grace ignored the turn, speeding off, and then veered into the left lane to pass a slow-moving truck ahead of her.

The caller lived in Wolfheze, a small town off a long roadway called the Parallelweg. Grace remembered that it was somewhere near that private golf course, not far from Ede.

Grace had been there exactly once, when she and Pieter had had a weird Sunday outing to the town, with lots of cameras in tow, because he thought the town might be a good subject for a photo documentary project. The place housed a nineteenth-century insane asylum, and later the town had added a home for the blind. It had some important World War II history, but she couldn't remember that part of the story.

How ironic that she was driving herself to an insane asylum. These days they would call it a "residential care setting for the mentally disabled," or maybe there was an even more "woke" expression for it now. Pieter had wanted to shoot there, but they had felt so strange walking through it, like they had arrived at the setting of *The Shining* or something. Pieter had looked up and pointed out the surveillance cameras on lamp-posts everywhere. Someone, surely, had been watching, but no one ever came to bawl them out and make them leave.

There was a little local history museum, a one-room brick building that had reminded her of an old village church, presided over by "the oldest man in the world," as Grace had called him when they got back into their car and drove back home. After they shook off the strangeness of the whole experience, Grace had confessed to Pieter that she'd found it quite illuminating—so many stories in a tiny little place. She'd encouraged Pieter at the time to pursue the photo documentary project, but he'd gotten the job in Syria instead, and they never went back to Wolfheze.

To the right, where she was supposed to have gotten off the highway, she saw tall trees beside the highway and the creek that ran below, just along the line of the road. This was the Otterlo side of the Hoge Veluwe, she thought. Maybe she should skip visiting this lady and just head out into the park to look for Karin right away?

"Rerouting," the GPS man announced, ever so politely defeated. "One moment, please. Rerouting. Rerouting."

Grace decided to go see the lady first. Otherwise, she would have no idea where to start looking in the park. It was a pretty massive forest, and it was late and she couldn't drive in till morning. Maybe this woman could lead her to the place where she'd found the shirt.

"In one hundred meters, turn left," said the GPS man finally. "Turn left in one hundred meters."

Just at the moment when she was about to lift her foot off the gas pedal and put her foot on the clutch to slow down, she heard a siren, high-pitched and shrill. The police. *Oh shit.* How fast had she been driving? She looked at the speedometer to see the needle pointing to 110 kph—way over the 80 kph limit. *Fuck. I can't stop now, she thought. It will take too much time. It's already taken too much time. I need to go find Karin.* She looked up and at that moment saw the exit sign reading, WOLFHEZE, 10 KM. So close. Right there already.

She depressed the clutch and moved into third gear, then into second, pressing on the brakes ever so slightly. But instead of stopping for the wailing police car behind her, she moved onto the exit ramp. *Fuck it,* she thought. *He's just going to have to follow me.* The off-ramp took her in a circle toward her destination. She looked in the rearview mirror to see what the police car was doing, and now its lights went on, full blare.

"Just give me a minute," she said to the cop car, even though he obviously couldn't hear her. "I'll tell you everything in a minute." The cop would have to understand.

Turning onto the road she needed, the cop car still trailing and blaring its siren and flashing its lights, Grace recognized the location. "In fifty meters, turn right." She was obedient now. *You see? We are in the same territory.* "Your destination is on the left." And there it was, so close to where she and Pieter had parked that time they'd visited this storied town.

He would be mad—she knew that even before she stopped her car. She made sure not to hesitate and raised her hands in the air as she saw the officer getting out of his car. She rolled down the window and screamed out, in Dutch: "Sorry, Officer. I can explain!"

The policeman who'd stepped out of the car behind Grace was furious. She could see it in his face, which was flushed and beaded with sweat when he leaned, just a little, toward her car window to get a better sense of what kind of person he was dealing with here.

"I can explain, Officer," said Grace, in her clearest Dutch, trying to sound as calm and sensible as possible. "I have a perfectly reasonable explanation."

CHAPTER 21

LITTLE RED

"Martijn, O-M-G," said Karin, looking up to see the figure of her stepfather scrambling down the side of the embankment to get to where she was standing. "I can't believe you found me!"

Even though Martijn was definitely not her favorite person, right now she was pretty happy to see him. When he reached her on the trail, she even ran toward him. She gave him a hug. That might have been the first time she'd ever done that.

"Don't worry," he said, patting her head. "I'm here. You don't have to be afraid anymore."

Karin pulled back. She hadn't been *so* scared. He smelled of sweat and something else—something she couldn't place—but it was kind of gross. It was like he'd been to the gym and then hadn't showered for days.

"I lost the others," she said. "Or they lost me. I don't know what happened. Are they all at the campsite already?" She assumed so.

"The others are fine," he said, stepping closer to put a hand on her shoulder. "All tucked into their sleeping bags

144

by now. I knew I had to get out here and find you, since we knew you were lost. And now I've found you."

Karin felt embarrassment creep over her. She was supposed to be the nature girl, the one who knew this park the best. But they'd had to send him out to get her, because she was the only one who'd gotten lost. "They all just kind of left me," she told Martijn. "First Dirk kind of beat us up, and then he and Margot just took off. Then I was with Lotte, but somehow she disappeared. Then I was on my own, and I thought I knew how to find the campsite. I was up in the sand drifts and then when it started to rain I ran into the forest, but then these people, these—"

"People?" Martijn was surprised.

"I don't know who they were, but they didn't look good. They didn't look human. Maybe it was just the darkness. Or maybe I just was really scared. They grabbed me and brought me back to their camp and told me that I needed to stay with them until morning. I thought they were going to do terrible things to me, but they didn't, they...they stole my backpack and they gave me a place to sleep. They were frightening, but I couldn't stay there..."

"Are you hurt?" Martijn put a hand on her other shoulder and looked her over, like, inspecting her, trying to see what had happened. "Did they hurt you? Are you okay?"

Karin pulled back, feeling uncomfortable. She wasn't *that* close with Martijn. He wasn't her mother.

"No, no, they didn't do anything, except steal my stuff. I think they were hungry. They were eating some food, some canned food, like maybe dog food or something like that. They didn't offer me anything and I didn't ask to eat it."

"That was smart of you."

"And then they told me that I should stay with them,

145

sleep with them there in their camp, until morning. I didn't want to say no; I didn't think I could say no. But I was really scared being there with them. They...they didn't look okay. I don't know how to say it, but their faces were all stretched out and I kept thinking they were maybe like zombies or vampires or...I know it sounds weird."

Martijn seemed to be thinking this over, like he could figure out who they were. Like he would know.

"But anyway, I got up and got away," said Karin. "I ran away just when they were woken up. Something else came into the camp, and then I ran..."

"Wait, what...?"

Karin didn't let him ask questions; she just wanted to get her story out. "And then I got out of the forest and I got here, and then there were wolves, and I had to scare them off. I got as big as I could get and I shouted, and they ran off. Just like my mom told me to do, and it worked! And then I was alone here, and I thought finally I knew how to get to the camp, and then you came, and then you're here..."

Karin suddenly felt herself to be dead tired, and without doing it on purpose she crumpled into Martijn's chest, her legs kind of buckling under her. All the energy that she had managed to muster to get this far seemed to seep out of her at once. She was exhausted.

Martijn grabbed her, trying to catch her before she fell. She slipped lower, but he pulled her back up and held her to his chest.

"There, there," he said, patting her head. *"Mijn Kleine Roodekapje,"* he added—*my Little Red Riding Hood.* "You got away from the Big Bad Wolf! That's impressive."

She felt the warmth of his body and realized how cold she had been. His strong arms around her back felt comforting.

But that smell. Something really rank. It wasn't just sweat; it was like...like it had a copper kind of edge to it. Kind of like a dead animal. But then also something else. What was it? Something weird and something else.

"I thought I was so strong, but really I'm weak," she said. "I'm tired and I'm scared and I just want to go home. I want to be home. I wish I could see Mom right now. I don't want to be here, doing this, anymore. I hate this dropping. I hate this whole trip."

"Don't worry," said Martijn. "Really, don't worry. We'll get you home. I'll get you home. We're not actually very far from the campsite, where Rutger and Riekje are waiting for us." He looked up, as if assessing the distance from where they were to where they needed to be, and then back down at her. "You rest for a moment," he said, gently lowering her to sit on a large rock, "and then we'll go there together."

That smell...Karin got another whiff of it as he leaned over to help her sit. There was something sickly sweet about it too. Like rose water. No, like rose water and cotton candy, a scent that came in a bottle in the shape of a swan. Was Martijn wearing Margot's perfume?

Karin nodded, looking up at him. His face looked really pale in the moonlight, and somehow different—somehow stranger than before. Like all the blood had been drained out of it. She couldn't quite put her finger on it. "Okay," she said. "Give me just a minute until I catch my breath."

A weird thought came into her head. What if Martijn had been captured by the ghouls too? What if they had bitten him and right now, before her eyes, he was turning into one of them? Like in those horror movies where outsiders come and take over the whole town by invading people's bodies one by one? What if they'd done that to Martijn? What if he

147

was already one of the outsiders and he was just pretending to be her stepdad?

The thought of that gave her the serious creeps, and she actually shuddered. Martijn saw it. Even in the dark, she could see the strange expression on his face, as if he was wondering what she was thinking. He crouched down and tried to give her a warm smile, but it had the opposite effect: She suddenly felt like she had to bolt. Martijn wasn't going to save her. She needed to get herself back to her mom. Her mom was the only one she could really trust. But what if the ghouls had gotten to her mom too?

CHAPTER 22

CULTURE CLASH

"I'm sorry I didn't stop. I know I should have, but I'm dealing with an...an...It might be an emergency."

"You were speeding," the policeman nearly yelled at her, his right hand on his belt. Did he used to have a gun there? Grace had read that the Dutch traffic police had been disarmed a few years ago. Had he even heard what she said? "License and registration." She could read every line in his face, etched with anger. "Now!" he said, without waiting for even a second.

"I'm getting it," she said, reaching for her purse to get out her license. "Please, Officer, let me explain."

"Remain silent, please," he said.

She handed over her license, motioning that she was going to reach into the glove compartment to get the registration, if that was okay with him. With a cop this angry, she didn't want to make a single false move, gun or no gun.

"Officer, I'm sorry," she added, handing him the registration.

"I need you to remain silent," he said again. Grace reasoned that this was more for his sake than for hers, so that he would calm down.

The anger lines in his face began to dissolve into soft, pudgy skin with old acne craters, and a scar on his chin was in the shape of a sickle.

"Ma'am," he started, "when you hear sirens from a police vehicle, you are required to stop your car on the side of the highway as quickly as possible." He reminded her, "Attempting to flee will only incur additional fines."

"I wasn't trying to flee, Officer," said Grace. "I didn't mean to ignore the sirens. I just—"

He didn't let her finish her sentence. "Where are you from?"

"I don't live that far from here," she started. "I was driving down here to see a woman..."

"No, I mean where do you come from? Your accent."

"Oh," said Grace, hardly understanding how this could possibly be relevant.

"Are you English?" he said. "England?"

"No, I'm American," she told him in Dutch. "I've been living here already for more than a decade. I—My husband is Dutch."

The officer glanced quickly at the house behind the car. "Where are you off to in such a hurry?"

"That's what I've been trying to tell you, Officer," she said, switching to English, since what was the point now of trying to speak in Dutch, which only slowed her down? "My daughter may be missing, and the person who lives in this house found an article of her clothing. That's why I drove here as fast as I could. It's no problem for me to pay the speeding ticket if you need to give me one, Officer. I understand that I was driving too fast. But you can't imagine how frightened I am right now. My daughter is only twelve."

"This is how the Americans do it," he said contemptuously.

"You just think you can do anything you want and pay your way out of it?"

"No! No, sir. That's not what I'm saying," she told him. "It's just that...it's an emergency."

"What kind of emergency?"

"My daughter. Her name is Karin. She's twelve and she went on a dropping with her Scout academy, here in Ede. I know it may sound stupid. She went into the Veluwe Park with a group of kids, and now she seems to be missing. The Scout leaders say they don't know where any of the kids are, and my husband, who is supposed to be one of the adult supervisors, isn't reachable on his phone. This woman called me and said her dog found Karin's T-shirt, and now I need to get inside that house right there and find out what the hell is going on."

She regretted cursing, and she realized that she was probably speaking way too fast for the police officer to understand her English anymore. He did pick up on one thing: "She went on a dropping?" he asked. "But you think she's missing? That's what a dropping is for, miss, to let the kids get a little bit lost for a while. They always come back safely. She'll find her way back, don't worry."

"No," said Grace, realizing that for him she was just another American woman who couldn't grasp the local customs. "No, it's not like that. It's really concerning. Maybe you can come into the house with me and talk to the woman here. She can explain..." Grace thought that since the woman who called her was Dutch, that might give her more credence.

"I don't need an explanation, miss," he said. "I'm sure there's nothing at all wrong with your daughter. She is having a good time with her friends and she'll be back tomorrow or the next day. We've seen lots of these droppings in the forest. The parents are a lot more freaked out than the kids are, especially the parents who aren't Dutch. I don't mean to be...to discriminate. I'm not sure of the word. We Dutch people do this all the time. She'll be having the time of her life, I promise you."

Grace could see that she wasn't going to be able to convince this man that the situation with Karin was serious. Anyway, he was just wasting her time at this point. She needed to get inside that house and talk to the woman who had called her. She didn't need to keep sharing information with this idiot.

"I'm going to have to give you a ticket," the cop said, drawing an electronic device out of his holster that looked like a video-game console.

"Great. Thanks," she said, as if she'd been waiting for this all day.

He tapped information into the console in a process that seemed interminable. He needed to scan her registration, fill in her phone number, her email address, her home address. How hard could it be to just tap in the fee and give her a receipt? "Do you want my bank card?" she asked. "I can pay it right away."

"No," he said absently, filling out his digital form. "It'll be sent to your home address and you can pay on our website."

"Great," she said. "Are we, um, done?"

He paused now, looking at her. It was as if he wanted to prolong the interaction as much as humanly possible, thought Grace. "There's probably some logical, simple explanation for what you're concerned about," he offered, speaking again in Dutch. "I know mothers can sometimes get very worried about their kids, especially if it's the first time she's away from home for the night. I remember when my son did a dropping for the first time. My wife was worried out of her mind. But everyone does it. We did it when we were kids. This is Holland. We do things a little differently than you do in America, but you'll get used to it."

Grace was in a mood to rant, and she would have at that moment if she didn't need to be done with this exchange as quickly as possible. Droppings may have been a nice tradition, but in today's world, was it so American of her to wonder whether it was wise to just let kids wander off at night into the biggest national park in the country? Someone might accuse her of being overly vigilant, and maybe she was. But it didn't matter how safe everything was supposed to be, or how good everyone was supposed to feel about tradition. Grace knew that things could go horribly wrong. And sometimes when you least expected it.

The device started whirring, and it spit out a tiny little stub of paper. He shoved the slip of paper through her open car window. "This is the number and date for your speeding ticket. In a few weeks you'll get a notice from the city traffic department with the official bill. You can send in the money or pay it online. You have an additional fine for trying to flee the scene of the crime."

"Fleeing the scene…" Grace stopped herself from arguing; that would not be at all helpful. She took the stub, and without waiting for his permission, she took off her seat belt and started to open the door of the car.

He wasn't budging, though. "By the way, if you don't hear from her in twenty-four hours, call 112. But I'm sure it'll all be resolved by then."

"Thanks, Officer," she managed to say through her fake smile. Then finally, finally, at long last, he turned around, got back into his car, and drove off.

CHAPTER 23

THE THUD

In the distance, she heard the howl of the wolf again, low and long. It didn't frighten Karin so much now, knowing how to scare him off. Martijn took it as a cue to start moving. "I think we'd better..." he said without finishing his sentence. He was still hovering over her.

She understood what he meant, but Karin didn't want to stand up. It was that smell on him, that icky rose water. Why did he smell like Margot?

Karin had heard everything that happened this morning, even though Martijn probably didn't know that. The kitchen was right underneath her bedroom. She hadn't been able to hear everything they said downstairs, just muffled, garbled words that drifted up through the floorboards. But she knew they were arguing, and then they got louder and louder. For a moment it had sounded like it might be over, but then all of a sudden they were really screaming and, like, wrestling or something. She could hear jostling in the kitchen, and her mother say, "Jesus, Martijn, get your hands off me." And then a scuffle. And then, "Let go of me!"

Then a crash and then the thud. Then this creepy silence. She must have been the only one home. Jasper had just left for football practice, and Frank, her other loathsome stepbrother, always slept over at his girlfriend's house now. If there had been sounds after that thud, even just normal sounds of people talking or walking around, she would have thought, *Okay, whatever.* But it was so quiet. She thought maybe her mom was dead.

Karin had run downstairs and, through the glass door to the kitchen, saw the two of them there. Her mom was sitting on the floor with her back against the kitchen cabinets, and Martijn was standing over her, his face red. Her mom wasn't dead, but she was crying and clutching her shoulder. Karin had ducked away, out of view of the door. Because what could *she* do?

Now, as Karin looked up at the face of her stepfather in the dark, her stomach convulsed. He looked so cold and remote, like he had been drained of all his blood. Maybe he was a vampire. Maybe he'd just come to suck the life out of them. They had been happy before he came along. Before her dad died. Before everything changed.

She began to clutch her abdomen as if she were suffering from cramps. "Ow," she said, not quite sure whether she was faking it for Martijn or whether her stomach really hurt. She did feel sick.

"Sounds like the wolves might be coming back," said Martijn, ignoring her and reaching down to help her up. Without waiting for her to agree, he hauled her to her feet. "We'd better get moving. Not that I think the wolves are coming for us or anything, but it'll be safer if we could all be at the camp together. It's really late."

There was that time when Karin had noticed red marks on her mother's wrist, a band of bruises that went all around her wrist, like a bracelet. Her mother had worn a long-sleeved shirt, one of those yoga shirts where you stick your thumbs through the holes, but Karin had seen it when her mother rolled up her sleeves to fill up Karin's bath.

Karin had asked her mom about it, and her mom had said she took the neighbor's dogs out for a walk and the leash had pulled on her wrist; the dogs had run so fast! Karin got excited to hear that some neighbors had dogs she didn't know about, but she was angry that her mom had not let *her* walk the neighbor's dogs...She knew how much Karin loved dogs. But the dogs were never mentioned again, and certainly there were no more opportunities for taking them out, even though Karin asked a lot of times. *Wow,* she thought now, *I'm really stupid.*

Now Martijn put his arm over her shoulder. She tried to pull away, but he held her close. Then he started walking, but not in the right direction. In the other direction.

Karin stopped. "Where are we going?"

"To the campsite, of course. To the other kids. To Rutger and Riekje. To your mom."

"I'm pretty sure it's in the other direction," she said, look-ing behind her. "That way. That's the way I was going."

"Oh no, Karin," he said. "You're just all turned around from your fall. It's this way."

"Are you sure?" Karin said. "I really thought it was over there..."

"Come on," he said, sounding tired, and grabbing her by the arm. "It's really late. And I'm getting impatient now."

She pulled her wrist out of his grip, taking her arm back. "Fine," she said. "We'll go the way you want to go. Just don't touch me, okay?"

He looked her over. "Wow," he said. "Not very ap-preciative, are we? If I hadn't come, you'd be lost in the woods by yourself, you know. But look, it's normal to be a little turned around, especially when you're scared. You can thank me for this later."

Thank you? Karin didn't say it out loud. But that's what she was thinking. *I'm never going to thank you for anything, you vampire.*

As they walked, in silence, Karin ahead, with Martijn behind her, like some kind of prison guard, she started to think about all the ways that their life had started to suck once Martijn came into it. Her mom used to be really relaxed and happy when her dad was around, but since she met Martijn, she was nervous, like, all the time. Her whole personality had changed. She got super anxious, and she'd jump on Karin if she did even the smallest thing wrong. She had never been like that before. She used to be really nice, really fun and funny. Even her mom's body kind of changed; she got weirdly thin, like rail thin, and not in a good way.

It sucked that they'd had to move into his house, with Jasper and Frank, who totally didn't want them there. They let her know all the time, calling her names and giving her nasty looks. They were pretty much always rude to her mother, but they were constantly torturing Karin, with all kinds of little tricks they thought were funny. Like they put a dead mouse in her closet one time, and another time a hamster in her underwear drawer. And they left things right outside her bedroom door so she'd trip when she walked out. One time they even dropped her toothbrush into the toilet and, when she told her mom, claimed she'd done it herself.

None of that mattered so much. Karin could protect herself. She was just really worried about her mom. Why did she let Martijn treat her like that? What was so great about him that they had to stay with him?

"Listen, Karin," said Martijn from behind her. "I know it may not be the best time to talk, 'cause it's late and we're both tired, but since we're here together..."

Oh no, thought Karin. *Here it comes.*

"I know it's been kind of a hard transition that we've had as a family," he started. "This last year. Your mom and I wanted to be all together, and I know that has been tough for you, because you miss your dad."

"It's not 'cause I miss my dad," Karin snapped.

"Okay, okay," he said. "I just meant, I can imagine that it might be really hard to start over with a new family after losing your dad. Maybe you didn't really have enough time to mourn before we—"

"Do we have to talk about this?" Karin said. "I don't need to talk about this."

"No," said Martijn. "No, we don't have to. Not if you don't want to." But then he continued anyway. "I've just been meaning to try to find some time alone with you. That's part of the reason I volunteered to do the dropping with you. I know this park was really important to you and your dad. It was kind of your place, right? You spent a lot of time alone together here. Must have been very bonding."

Karin couldn't believe this. Was he really going to be jealous of her relationship with her dad? That was so lame. "It's, like, the middle of the night," she said. "I'm not really in the mood to talk."

"That's true," he said. "But when else do we have this kind of opportunity?"

"O-M-G, are you *serious*? What do we have to talk about?"

"Oh, lots of things. Lots of things," he said. "For example, I want to tell you that I feel really sorry about what happened to your father. He was a good man trying to do something important in the world, and he got killed for the wrong reason. That shouldn't have happened."

"You don't have to say that," Karin said. "You don't have to apologize. People don't have to apologize all the time. It wasn't your fault, obv."

He was silent for a moment. "I know you guys spent a weekend together out here, camping together, before he left the last time for Syria. Was that nice? Do you have good memories of that?"

There was something really irritating about the way he wanted to know so much about them, but she had a little voice of her mom in the back of her head saying, *Why can't you open up to him just a little bit? He's really trying, Karin. He may be clumsy about it, but he's trying.*

"Yeah, it was nice," said Karin, letting the memories of that final trip flood back into her mind again. "He loved this forest so much. He tried to do a lot of nature photography here. We came here a lot. Actually, we just left our spot. The place where we camped that last time. Also other times. That's where we always saw the mouflons. That's why I knew where we were just now. Where we ran into each other back there? That was my dad's favorite camping spot."

Martijn did something really weird then. He grasped her wrist again, for no reason at all.

"Where we just were?" he said. "The place we just left?"

It was a tight grip. Too tight. She thought about her mom's wrist and the bruise band, and the supposed dogs her mom had said she walked, which she didn't walk.

Karin glared at him while she tried to shake her arm loose. "Give me my arm back."

"Tell me," he said. "Where?"

159

CHAPTER 24

CALLER

The caller's house had a fence around it and a cobblestoned path that led to a quaint little cabin that looked like a gingerbread house from a fairy tale. It was painted dark brown, with a whimsical bright-yellow door, yellow trim, and the shape of a heart cut into the front door. Grace stepped onto a welcome mat that was shaped like a gingerbread house and let the surreal element of the moment touch her for a second.

She rang the bell, which chimed with a cheerful sound of reindeer bells. Immediately, she heard loud barking. It was not just one dog but many—maybe dozens of dogs. Some of them seemed to be throwing their bodies up against the front door to try to open it themselves. She heard scratching and falling.

It wasn't long before the door swung open, and she saw a human figure pushing through the dogs amassed by the entrance. "Hush, now," the human said. Grace couldn't see her that well because of a screen door between them, but it seemed to be the woman. "Calm down, everyone. Quiet." The dogs barked and yelped and jumped while the woman patted their heads.

Grace watched her maneuver. She could see that the woman was older than she'd anticipated, maybe in her late sixties or seventies. Her hair was big and round and silvery, reminding Grace of a halo in those medieval paintings, sort of hovering behind her head. The woman's eyes were hidden behind large square-framed glasses and looked tired.

"It's the middle of the night," Grace said. "I'm so sorry to disturb you."

"Don't apologize. I understand the urgency."

Having pacified the dogs to some degree, the woman turned her attention to Grace, peering through the screen. Grace could see that she was very tall, with broad shoulders like a man's, and she listed just a little to the left. She thought: Julia Child. A Dutch Julia Child. Grace imagined her, for another second, holding a meat cleaver up over lots of headless raw chickens, and smiling a big, mischievous smile.

The woman drew up her glasses to rest them on the top of her head. The expression on her face was serious as she finally opened the door. "I'm Maaike Bol," the woman said. "You must be Grace."

"Yes, Grace. Grace Hoogendijk," she added. "I came as quickly as I could, but maybe too quickly. I got pulled over for speeding."

"Oh, I should have warned you. They are always patrolling that exit. Did you get a ticket? Please come in." Maaike pushed the screen door wide, and the dogs started barking again. "Don't worry about them. They're all sweet, friendly dogs. Susje here might jump up on you, but I just clipped her claws this morning. You can also just push her back down and she'll obey."

Grace took a step forward tentatively while making a mental inventory of the hounds: a lean, shaggy dog; a brown spotted dog with long ears; a pair of small sausage dogs; a scruffy terrier; and a big black Labrador. Six in all.

The little house was as quaint on the inside as it was on the outside, with mismatched antique furniture and lots of porcelain figurines everywhere.

"I know that I alarmed you," Maaike said, ushering Grace into the living room, past the sniffing canines. "I was debating as to whether it was a good idea to get involved, but that's me. If I see something that looks strange or suspicious, I like to help. If I were the mother, I'd want to know."

Maaike had a matronly way about her, with her eggplant-and-squash-colored dress made of a thick organic cotton. On one foot she had a soft gray sneaker and on the other foot, her left foot, she had an enormous navy-blue boot, covering a plaster cast.

"Oh, you've hurt your foot," said Grace. "Is it broken?"

"Yes, yes, it's a ridiculous story," Maaike began, ushering Grace into her house. "You know how one bad turn becomes another—in this case quite literally. My poor dear husband, Wim, who is now seventy-two years old, had to have his hip replaced. He's needed it for a long time, but finally the pain got too bad and the orthopedist said it was a must. So I took him into the hospital on Tuesday, and we realized just after he was admitted that we had forgotten all his diabetes medications, and so I had to rush back home and get all that. And so I was leaving the hospital, and I guess I was just in too much of a rush because when I got outside there was a young boy there, and he had a skateboard, and I guess he was just rolling up and down the street for fun. Well, at some point he skated past me and then he fell into me—or maybe I ran into him, I can't say—and he fell off the board, and then I tripped on the board, and there we were, the two of us lying on the pavement together. Luckily, we were right there at the hospital already. So they took us inside and then did some X-rays, and it turned out that I got the worse of it. He was okay with just some bruises and scratches—you know how kids' bodies just bounce back from everything—and I had to get this cast for my ankle. But it's not as bad as it looks. I can still walk on it."

Grace was selfishly wondering how this woman with a lame foot would hold her up. "It seems you must be doing pretty well with it if you went for a walk in the woods with the dogs already," she said hopefully.

"The dogs need to be walked a few times a day, and with my husband in the hospital, who else can do it? Plus, they say it's good for my recovery."

"And your husband? How did the surgery go?" Grace was doing her best to be at least minimally polite, in spite of her drive to get moving.

"He's all right. He got sick from the anesthesia, but they say the operation was a success."

Grace followed Maaike into a living room with a white tile floor and baroque-looking furniture spaced around a coffee table covered with ceramic figurines. A figurine of a woman in a nineteenth-century dress holding a parasol. A figurine of a woman in eighteenth-century costume reaching down to pat a tiny dog. A ceramic cat climbing up onto a ceramic birdbath, where a tiny ceramic bird was about to take flight.

They moved at Maaike's pace into the kitchen, followed

by all the dogs, where Grace could see a red bucket on the counter. "I put it up here so the dogs couldn't get to it again," said Maaike, reaching to show the bucket to Grace.

She could immediately recognize Karin's T-shirt inside, with white and pink stripes and with a pink sequined star right in the middle. It was one of those "interactive" T-shirts they sold at H&M. Grace had an image in her mind of Karin swiping her hand over it, up and down, to make it change colors. Silver up, pink down. Anyone could have bought it; lots of kids walked around in identical H&M wear at school.

Grace reached into the bucket and took out the shirt, bending back the collar to find the tag, which read "Karin 0641420787," Grace's own phone number. That was inarguable. She raised the shirt to examine it. Right in the center of it was a huge dark stain of brownish red, and lots of holes punctured around the star.

She felt suddenly faint and grabbed on to the counter to wait for her head to stop spinning. Maaike's hand came to rest on her back, steadying her. "The gashes are from Jezebel's teeth," said Maaike. "I think."

Grace let her head clear and took a deep breath. That stain could be blood, but it could also be something else—red paint or ketchup or tomato sauce.

She brought the shirt to her nose to smell it, and got a whiff of something truly awful. It didn't smell like blood per se; it didn't have that slightly coppery scent. It smelled like something rotting, chemical, like the kind of toxic solution you'd use to clean out a really mildewed bathroom. It reminded her a bit of rotten eggs, sulfur. It may not have been blood, but it certainly wasn't only something child friendly, like ketchup or tomato sauce.

"I need you to show me where you found this," said Grace.

"Of course," Maaike said. "But do you think we should call someone? The police?"

Grace thought of the conversation she'd just had with the highway patrolman and anticipated how contacting the cops would only slow her down. Karin wasn't technically missing yet, because she was scheduled to be on the dropping until tomorrow afternoon. And Grace knew this was not the shirt Karin had been wearing when she went out this afternoon. So at least that was something—something slightly less worrying. It was an extra shirt that she and Karin had packed in her zebra backpack this morning while sitting on the living room floor—Grace was sure of that. It also seemed that whatever this fluid was on the shirt might not be blood, so maybe the cops would not help anyway.

"No, not now," she said. "I've got my cell phone; if we find something we'll call them." But as she said it, she swiped her phone to check the battery. She was already down to 23 percent.

Grace would have asked to charge the phone then, but there was no time.

"We can take my car," Maaike said. "The dogs are used to it, and I know the way to the place where we had our walk earlier. Is that all right with you?"

"Yes, of course. Can you drive with..." Grace looked down at Maaike's booted foot.

"Oh, it's no problem. Thank God it was my left foot, not my right."

The foot didn't turn out to be the limiting factor. It soon became clear that Maaike didn't go anywhere without *all* of her dogs. She was less their owner than their pack leader, thought Grace, watching her try to get them all clipped into their leashes while balancing on one foot and the heel of her huge blue boot. Grace was becoming increasingly anxious. She asked Maaike if she had flashlights and a first-aid kit, and if she did, if it would be okay if Grace got them. Maaike instructed her where to find everything while she wrestled the Labrador into a reflective vest.

"They love to be out there once they're out there," Maaike told her apologetically. "It's just a matter of getting all their noses pointed in the same direction." The two sausage dogs had run around her, so her ankles were now tied up in leashes, threatening to topple her.

Grace didn't have much of a plan at this point, except to get out there with flashlights, somewhere near where the dog had found the shirt, and to start calling Karin's name. She figured that if Karin was hurt and lying somewhere out there by herself, at least she could hear her mother's voice. But what if she was unconscious? Grace could only hope to come across her body with the flashlight in the darkness. Just the thought of that made her shiver. "Which one is the hunting dog?" she asked Maaike. "The brown one?"

"Jezebel," said Maaike, putting her hand out to pat the snout of a large brown dog, with dangling brown-and-white spotted ears. "This one. She's a naughty girl. But she's very good at finding things."

"If we give her the piece of clothing to smell and then send her out looking for my daughter, will she do it?" she asked, now thinking, she felt, with a bit of a clear head.

"We can certainly give it a try."

She asked Maaike, "Do you have some kind of bullhorn or something that could amplify my voice?"

"No, I'm afraid that I don't," Maaike replied, and Grace could see that she was now unraveling the leashes from around her ankles and starting to break free. At last she was jangling her car keys, walking toward the front door of her house.

CHAPTER 25

OFF COURSE

"We'd better go back," he said.

"What do you mean?" she said. "You said you knew the way. You said it was this way, even when I told you it was the other direction."

"Well, I am sure you know this park better than me," he said. "You've been here so many times before. I'm new. I am just getting to know the forest."

This change in attitude was really odd. First he knew where he was going and then suddenly he didn't? Suddenly it was her job to show *him* the way?

She was going to argue, but then he just started to walk back to where they'd come from, now picking up speed. She had to run to catch up with him.

"Uuuuuuugh!" she cried. "Stop. I don't even want to go to the campsite now. Can't we just go home? Can't we just go back to the parking lot and skip the rest of this? I'm tired of all this, and I want to give up. Can't we just call Mom and have her pick us up? I give up. It's not worth it."

He stopped and turned back to look at her. He seemed to be inspecting her like a robot that had just malfunctioned. "Karin, giving up?" he said.

"Yeah, well, it's okay to give up sometimes."

"What would be the fun of that?" he said. "Come on. No whining, Karin. You show me the way back."

"Ugh, fine."

They retraced their steps for at least ten minutes until they got back to the mouflon spot. She saw the two boulders and the tree, and the place where they'd camped that last time, and other times before that. It felt nice to be someplace she recognized again, but she expected they would just keep walking past it in the right direction this time.

"Here," she said. "This was our camping spot. So if you think about it, the campsite has to be northwest of here, which means it's that way, right?" She started off in that direction.

"Very good, Karin," said Martijn. But he didn't look in the direction she figured the camp must be. He just stood there, looking at the spot where she and her dad had camped, like he was seeing it for the first time, even though they'd been here just before.

"Could you show me exactly where you would set up camp? Around here somewhere?" He made a circle motion with his hand. For some reason Martijn had this creepy way of being particularly interested in everything her dad had done. If his name came up, he always wanted to know more, to ask more questions. She'd thought it would be the opposite—why would a second husband be so interested in his wife's first husband? Karin could only reason that he was probably jealous that her dad had been more important to her mom, and he was trying to figure out how to be more like him.

Karin was so tired. "I mean, I don't know why you care so much."

"I just want to know where you camped. No reason."

"Are you jealous or something?"

Martijn seemed really impatient now, glaring at her in the darkness. "Show me where you set up camp, Karin."

He was really irritating when he got this way. "I'll tell you if it's so important to you," she said. "There, we'd pitch our tent about there." She pointed to the place under the tree.

"Tell me more," he said. "How you got here, where you put your stuff."

"What? Why?"

"Just tell me."

Karin had no clue why he wanted to know this, but she was too tired to argue. "We always parked our car at the Otterlo gate, and then we'd bike down here with our gear. We always set up our tent over there, under that tree," she said, whirling around to show him. "We made our fire there. We'd go to sleep, like, right after the sun set. Even him. So in the morning we could wake up really, really early and watch the mouflons. We must have seen hundreds of mouflons here. He liked to photograph them when they were in a herd, and they only came here when it was really silent, so we—"

"The tent went here?" he said, walking to the spot, like a land surveyor or something. Like he was going to build a house right there. Or put up a statue or something.

"Yeah, about there," she said. "What's this all about?"

Martijn started to do the weirdest thing then. He took a small shovel out of his backpack, shined a flashlight on the ground at the base of the tree, then dropped to his knees and started digging.

"I thought we were going to the campsite," Karin said. "Why are you doing that?"

"I'm looking for something," said Martijn. "Something that belongs to me."

"You left something here? Or you lost something? I don't understand."

"Don't ask questions if you know what's good for you, Karin. Just keep quiet." The coldness of his voice and the way his eyes glared at her—without a hint of pity or patience—suddenly terrified her. It occurred to her that he *had in fact been* bitten by one of those ghouls.

She stood stock-still and dared not say another word. She kept her eyes on him, though, hoping he might soften, crack a smile. It would all turn out to be a big joke. *"Ha ha, gotcha!"*

But no. The more she watched him, the more she saw that he was involved in something completely different from the dropping. He wasn't here for her. He was here for some other reason. He was searching for something, digging for something. He had wanted to find her not to save her but to get her to lead him here.

Karin had the sudden instinct to run, and she took a few steps backward before she suddenly whipped around. But as she was just about to sprint, at nearly exactly the same moment, Martijn lurched up from where he was digging and tried to grab her. He fell over and caught her ankle instead, holding it fast and tight. Then she fell, face-first, into the dirt.

"What are you doing...?" Karin tried to say, but she couldn't get the words out. She was panting and trying to squirm out of his grip. The more she did, the tighter he clenched. What was he doing? Why was he trying to prevent her from moving?

She tried to lift herself off the ground, but he pulled

himself on top of her, pinning her to the dirt. A kind of wrestling move. It shocked her. What was he going to do to her? Was he going to try to assault her? Was this what he did to her mother?

"Just stay still," Martijn said. He was panting too, breathing hard, trying to catch his breath. He pushed himself up to kneeling, and put one knee on her waist to keep her pinned. They continued to struggle until she gave up and went limp.

"You're hurting me, you know," she said.

He nodded. He did know.

"You're obviously not taking me to the campsite," she said.

"Okay, you win," he said, suddenly very matter-of-fact. "No, we're not going to the campsite. Well, maybe we'll go later. But we're not going until I find the photographs. I just need to know where he buried them. That's all. I need you to show me. I need you to help me find them. He said he'd left them in the woods. They must be buried where he camped. I'm pretty sure you know where they are too."

Karin had no idea what he was talking about. No idea. It was the strangest thing she had ever heard, and yet he seemed to be talking about something she was supposed to understand completely. "Buried photographs?" she said. "What are you talking about? Who?"

"Your father," he said. "Good old Pieter Hoogendijk. Come on, Karin, don't tell me you don't know. I know he told you. I know you're the only person who knows."

"What?" Karin was beyond herself. She felt like he was accusing her of being some kind of accomplice to a crime she didn't commit. To a crime she hadn't even ever heard about. "You think my dad buried photographs? Out here? Why would he do that? Why would he tell me?"

"I didn't believe him at first, of course," said Martijn. "It did seem stupid, like he was trying to send me off course. But now I've searched every other conceivable place. All his storage facilities, all his files, all his computers, all his everything. Then I thought: What if he wasn't shooting digitally? What if he was shooting on old-fashioned film? He liked to do that sometimes, didn't he? He did his nature photography on film."

This much Karin did know. Her father had an old-fashioned side. He was used to using film, and he liked to shoot sometimes in black-and-white. And he liked to develop his rolls of film in the darkroom at home. He'd even taught Karin how to do it. She wasn't allowed to put her hands in the chemicals, but she was allowed to put them in the final bath and hang them up to dry, using clips that he'd attach to strings hanging from the ceiling.

"This was where you came on the last trip you took with your father," Martijn said. "You were determined to come back. That was part of the reason, wasn't it? He buried the negatives out here. Maybe he even told you about what the photos were of?"

Now Karin thought Martijn had really gone off the deep end. What kind of person would bury negatives in the forest? Why would he tell his ten-year-old daughter about it and not anyone else? Everything Martijn was saying seemed to make no sense. But he was so sure of it.

"No." Karin shook her head. "No, he didn't tell me about anything like that. He didn't tell me about what he was doing. He wasn't like that. I was just a kid. Why would he tell me?"

Martijn looked like he maybe believed her for a moment. He seemed, at least, to consider what she said. She had to convince him that she really didn't know—because she *really* didn't know—what he was talking about.

"Because he had to tell someone," said Martijn. "And it seems he didn't tell your mother anything."

Karin thought of all the times Martijn had hurt her mother. Was this what it was all about? Was he trying to get something out of her too? Her mind skipped a beat. All kinds of thoughts came flooding in. All kinds of thoughts she didn't even want to think.

She asked him, "Did you ever actually love my mother at all?"

CHAPTER 26

LETTING JEZEBEL LOOSE

The dogs leapt out of the car and ran into the park, pulling Maaike behind them. She nearly tripped in her boot. They were all on leashes that connected to a big metal ring, so she could hold them all at once, but in their excitement, they catapulted her forward. Grace was surprised by their level of energy—after all, it was the middle of the night.

There was a slanted wooden gate that stood at the edge of the forest and opened onto a dirt clearing. Just beyond that was a post that had all kinds of markings on it, indicating which trails went in which directions. Once they were inside the park, Maaike leaned forward and unclipped the dogs from their leashes, one by one, and off they ran.

Jezebel was the last one on the lead. Maaike motioned to Grace to give her Karin's shirt. Without any further discussion, she held it up to the dog's nose and let her get a good long whiff. "That should do it," she said to Grace. "She'll take us there."

Then she let Jezebel go. The dog behaved strangely at first, just running in circles around the dirt clearing, not seeming to know which direction to go. Then she ran up and down one trail and back to Maaike, like the other dogs were doing, and leapt up on her master. Maaike held out the shirt again, and Jezebel barked, just once. She chose a trail and ran off quickly in that direction, and Maaike and Grace nodded to each other before they turned on their flashlights and followed. The rest of the dogs also came along, running up and down the path, up ahead and then back, playfully, with no sense of the terrible dread Grace was feeling.

They'd been following Jezebel for about ten minutes already, shining flashlights into the dark, when they heard Jezebel wailing.

"I guess it worked," Maaike said as she picked up her pace. Grace began to run, charging ahead of the older woman. As she did, she felt a stab of pain in her chest—was it fear and dread, or just her heart worn out by the strain? She was nearly breathless when she pressed through some branches to find the dog digging furiously with her paws in the dirt under a cluster of trees. No sign of Karin there.

Grace stopped and shone her flashlight all around the floor of the forest, seeing garbage everywhere. Plastic bottles, large ones and small ones, and giant tin cans strewn about the place, lots of plastic bags. A large green tarp was half suspended from the branches of a tree, and half fallen into the dirt. There were also filthy sleeping bags, cups and knives, and metal plates strewn about, and industrial-size containers labeled ACETONE and WEED KILLER.

Maaike caught up with her, breathing heavily, and her flashlight also scanned the scene. "Looks like someone has been living here," she said.

They wandered around the empty campsite, seeing the now-dead campfire, its embers seemingly doused by water. There were all kinds of chemicals everywhere and a concerning amount of garbage. It was clear that some people had been here pretty recently. Maybe even hours ago. Where had they gone? Did they leave or were they chased out?

"I think it's a meth lab," said Grace. "I've been reading about this in the papers. They're using various forests for it these days." Her heart began to sink—this was frightening, but it held no clue to Karin's whereabouts.

Maaike went over to inspect what Jezebel was digging up. She was wrestling something out of the dirt with her teeth. "Is this..." she started to say as Grace turned to see what the dog had unearthed from her hole. "Is it...?"

"Karin's backpack," Grace said as Jezebel lifted the zebra-striped bag in her teeth. "She was here." Grace felt her stomach drop. At the very least, Karin had been out here with some frightening people. Why? Had the other kids been here too? Or just Karin? What on earth had she been doing here? Had they kidnapped her? What did they plan to do with her?

The obvious next question didn't need to be said aloud, but Grace said it anyway. "So where is she?"

"Let's call the police," said Maaike. "We'd better call now."

Grace grabbed her phone out of her jacket pocket and was about to dial when the phone rang instead. It was Rutger calling. Maybe he had news. She accepted the call and held it to her ear.

"Hello, Grace. I wanted to let you know that one of the children has arrived. Only one, but that's something. Dirk is here. He found his way to the camp."

"Only Dirk?" said Grace. "What about the girls?"

"So far it's only him," said Rutger, slowing his speech so that Grace knew she needed to listen carefully. "He is very shaken. He says that he was with Margot, but the two of them went off on their own and left Lotte and Karin behind. He is the only one who has made it here. Have you reached your husband yet?"

"Left the other two behind? Where?" Grace was trying to take this in. She was sure she hadn't heard him right.

"I guess they were trying to have a private, um, moment. They're thirteen—I don't know. Sometimes kids do that. Your husband, Martijn," said Rutger. "He was supposed to follow the kids. Did you talk to him?"

"No, I've been calling him for hours," she said. "I can't reach him. I can't understand why."

Rutger paused for a pregnant moment. "Dirk says that Martijn found him with Margot—they were not where they were supposed to be. I think they were doing something…something sexual. Martijn apparently separated them and sent Dirk ahead on his own. Martijn told him he would accompany Margot to the camp because she should not be alone out there. But they have not arrived. No one else has arrived yet."

"What?" Grace was dumbfounded. She was beginning to understand that the spool of thread that held this whole event together had unraveled. How far had it unraveled? Was there no one in charge? No one was where they were supposed to be. "What?"

"Your husband was with Margot, but…" He started to repeat his story, as if she hadn't heard him.

"No, no, I heard what you said. I just don't understand; I don't understand what all of this means. Martijn was with Margot? But they aren't there yet. They didn't make it to the campsite. What about Riekje?" asked Grace. "Did you hear from her?"

"No," Rutger said with a deep sigh. "Nothing. I've been

calling and calling her too. She's not answering her phone, and she didn't come back to camp. Right now it's just Dirk and me here. I need to make sure he's okay, get him warm and safe, and in the meantime, I'll keep trying her."

"Did Dirk say anything else about what happened? Where he was when he saw Martijn? Is he talking about what happened to him?"

"No, he's very shook up. I'm giving him some food now, and I'll try to sit down with him when he's a little more, well, calmer. Something seems to have spooked him badly. He seems like he is kind of in shock, I think. I'm as confused as you are. I don't understand what's happening. And we don't have Margot or Lotte or Karin. And now both of the supervisors are missing as well. So things have gone really wrong somehow, I have to admit. I'm sorry about this, Grace. I'm calling the Scout organization to see if they can send out some help. Maybe you can drive down."

"I'm already in the Veluwe," said Grace. "I told you that this woman called me on the phone because she found Karin's shirt. So I drove down here. We found the place where Karin lost it; we discovered her backpack here too. But she's not here."

"Oh?"

"It is a strange place, I think a meth lab. I really don't know what it is, but it's creepy. There's no one here, but there were people here recently. I can't tell if they took Karin with them or if she got away. I can't see any signs of any of the others here, but there is a lot of garbage. Maybe they are attacking people in the park. I don't know. I don't know what to think. It's all very upsetting. We were just about to call the police when you called me."

"Oh Jesus," said Rutger. "I don't understand what's going on. Should we come to you?"

"No, stay where you are, in case anyone shows up there."

"Okay, but we need to coordinate. Can you try your husband again?"

"I will try again. I have been trying and trying," said Grace. "Dirk says he was with Margot when he saw him last?"

Rutger sounded like he had pulled his mouth away from the receiver; she could hear him speaking to Dirk in the background. "Yes, he said Margot sprained her ankle and Martijn was going to help her walk to camp. He says he told Dirk to go ahead."

Grace felt herself recoil inwardly. *Oh God.* She felt as if invisible hands were creeping up her throat, trying to strangle her. Could Martijn have something to do with this? Or was it something else that had somehow gotten to all of them? Whoever was here at this weird campsite? They had obviously had contact with Karin. But could they have somehow had contact with everyone else too?

"I don't understand," said Rutger.

"Neither do I," said Grace, and she thought at that moment that she might just start to cry. "It's clear only that something has gone terribly wrong. I'm hanging up to call the police and then I'll call you back."

"Yes," said Rutger. "I agree. I'll call the Scout program to see if we can get some extra hands out here. I'll also contact the other parents. You call the police."

CHAPTER 27

CONFESSIONS

Karin's wrists hurt a lot. They were tied behind her back and to a tree. It was the tree where she and her dad had pitched their tent. Martijn had used some kind of really prickly rope to fasten her hands together, and her arms were pushed up against the hard bark of the tree. She squirmed and wriggled to try to free herself, but it only tore at her skin.

Martijn seemed to have gone actually nuts. He had this headlamp he'd put on, and he was bent over, on his knees, wildly digging in the ground around where she had said her dad had pitched their tent. He kept asking her questions, like she was supposed to know something about something. She told him what she could—where they had put this and that—but she really didn't know what he wanted. He kept saying that she had to know more, but she didn't know anything.

"I promise, I swear, I don't know what you're looking for," she said. "Please, Martijn. Can't you untie me? I won't go anywhere, I won't. I will stay with you here until you find what you're looking for. I promise."

"There's no point in going to the campsite anyway," he said. "No one is there."

"What do you mean, no one is there? They're all waiting for us."

He stopped digging, stood up, and came toward her. She turned her face away, thinking he might smack her. He didn't. He just stood there looking at her, *staring* at her, with his headlamp shining into her eyes. That hurt her eyes. It blinded her too.

"I swear," she said again, this time starting to cry. "I swear I don't know what this is about."

"I believe you," he said. "I believe that you don't know. Or maybe you think you don't know. Maybe he told you but you don't remember. That might be it."

It was like he thought if he just stared at her, shining that light in her eyes, she would suddenly remember something she had forgotten. But all she could think was that she wished her dad were here right now to save her. "My dad was my dad," she said. "He just was a dad. He didn't tell me his secrets, ever. He protected me."

That seemed simple enough. And anyway it was so long ago that they were here last. Martijn was completely losing his mind.

"Maybe if you tell me what this is all about…" Karin started. She had to think about ways to get him to let her go. If he would talk to her, maybe he would calm down. "He did tell me some things, but maybe not what you think he told me…"

Martijn tore the headlamp off his head. His eyes looked wild. "I really don't want to harm you, Karin," he said. "But if I don't find these photos, I'm in trouble. I'm in a lot of trouble. I need these photographs he took because they help prove my innocence."

Karin shook her head. She didn't understand any of

this. He didn't make sense. "Maybe he meant it, like, metaphorically..." Karin started. "Like not really buried but, like, put away somewhere. Why would someone bury something in a forest?"

Martijn flashed his eyes back at her. "You're pretty clever for a twelve-year-old, huh? Metaphorically... You think that hasn't occurred to me? I have looked everywhere else where they might have been stashed. I have found all his old files, all his old computer files, all his digital photo archives... I have searched for two years. More..."

Karin felt her mind clicking little pieces into place. Is this why he always seemed so interested in everything that had to do with her dad? Is this why he was always asking her weird questions? Is this why he always asked her about her father when her mother wasn't there? It wasn't jealousy, she thought. It was like something out of a murder mystery... Maybe she had to start thinking faster, to start thinking like a murder-mystery writer. Or like a detective. Like Miss Marple in those Agatha Christie books. Like Nancy Drew in the series her mom gave her. Like Harriet the Spy.

"If you tell me," she started, "maybe if you tell me exactly what happened and what he took from you and why he had these photographs, I could help you. It was a long time ago that we were here, but maybe if you tell me what it's about, I could start to remember. It could jog my memory. I could help you find them and protect yourself."

He looked at her in an odd way, obviously not sure if she was trying to trick him. He glanced down and then back at her, as if deciding that it was better to try this approach than not to.

"I wasn't always working as an accountant," he started

to explain. "Before I did that, I had another job. I was in foreign affairs. Do you know what that means?"

"Yeah," she said. "We do current events in school. I read the newspapers."

"I know," said Martijn. "I know you do."

"So, what... Does that mean you were also working in Syria, like my dad?"

"Not there, no. I didn't go there, but I worked for the government department that deals with things in that part of the world," he said. "I was involved with the government's... operations."

Karin remained silent. She knew that if she didn't talk, he would probably talk more. Maybe he would somehow tell her something that would allow her to figure out what to do. In the meantime, whenever he looked away from her, she tried to work on the knots behind her back.

"The Dutch are part of an international coalition that wants the Syrian government out of power," he said. "The government of President Assad."

"I know a lot about Syria," Karin said. "I've read a lot about it since my dad died."

"Well, then you know that it is a bad regime, killing its own citizens," he said. "The Dutch originally had the idea that by supporting rebel groups, antigovernment organizations fighting the regime, we could help take them down."

"Yes, I know that part."

"One of the groups our government was supporting got away from us, you could say. They weren't clean. They turned on us. This group turned out to be Salafist, which means they were anti-imperialists, which means... which means they were jihadists—do you know what that means?"

"I know what 'jihadist' means," Karin said. "All the

papers said the jihadists killed my father. I know what it means." Karin thought, basically, that jihadists wanted all Europeans to be dead, and that's why when they saw her father they shot him. Just like that. They never asked what he was doing there or if he was helping anyone or doing anything positive for their country; they just didn't like who he was, what he represented.

"Yes, well, that was them," said Martijn. "That's the simplest way to put it."

Karin thought about this, what she knew from the papers and what she'd heard from her mother, and what she'd learned in school.

"What do you mean? The Dutch government doesn't fund jihadists," she said.

"It did," he said. "It did back then, without knowing it. The idea was to support anti-Assad rebel groups to try to diminish his power, and we didn't know that they were jihadists at the time."

"Is that who shot my dad? Is that what you're saying? Someone paid by the Dutch government?"

He started pacing around in a circle. He was trying to explain himself. "It wasn't clear from the beginning that they were jihadists, but we heard that might be a possibility. My job at the time was to do an investigation, to find out what was going on there. That was why I hired your father. We wanted someone who already knew the country, who had ways of getting around, who understood the politics. Your dad had spent a lot of time there, and because he was a photojournalist, he had access, he could do things other people couldn't do."

Karin wriggled against the tree, trying to maneuver so she could at least move a little. Her hands hurt so much. She tried to feel the tree to see if it had any sharper pieces of bark that she could use to latch on to the rope and loosen it.

"What does that mean, you *hired* my dad? My dad worked for newspapers and magazines. He didn't work for the government."

"Mostly he worked for newspapers and magazines," said Martijn. "But he also worked for me. He worked for the government, doing some work for us."

Karin felt the weirdest thing behind her. It was sharp, but not the way pieces of bark are sharp. More like the way something metal is sharp. Like the corner of a box made out of metal. She couldn't see it, of course, because her back was to the tree, but when she felt around, it did seem like it was not something you find in nature. And it seemed to be tucked into a hole in the trunk of the tree.

She had to keep Martijn talking. "What are you saying, then? Are you telling me my dad was a spy? That he was a spy? You're a liar. He was not like that."

Karin had heard too much dumb stuff from too many people about her dad and Syria and the stupid war over there and what he was doing there and accusations that he worked for ISIS or for the CIA or whatever…It was enough. Her mom had told her to ignore it all. It was all a big lie. "You're either a liar or you're just an asshole."

Even though Martijn was like some weird, crazy stranger now, he suddenly looked like he totally understood her. He looked like he was trying to tell her something. "I know it's really hard to understand, Karin," he said. "It will take a long time for you to really understand it. Maybe you never will."

"I don't want to hear any more," she said, thinking now that she had to get his eyes off of her. She had to figure out what this sharp thing was behind her back. A metal box hidden in the tree. Could it actually be what he was searching for? "You're just going to lie to me, like everyone else."

"I need you to help me or else I'm going to get in a lot of trouble. The photographs your father took could exonerate me. They'll show that we knew before the government knew, and that we tried to inform them. I need the photos or the negatives. If I don't find them, I'll be arrested. I might go to prison. I don't know what will happen. They'll definitely put my name in the paper and expose me as the one who paid off the jihadists. That's why I want to tell you now, so you'll hear it from me. Karin, I have been trying to find a way to tell you for a long time..."

"Tell me that my dad was a spy? I don't even believe that. That pictures he took could save you? But they didn't save him?"

"He wasn't a spy, Karin," said Martijn. "He was helping the government to get information. That was good. We needed to know. Your father was doing the kind of work he wanted to do—to help reveal the truth."

"But the jihadists found out and that's why they killed him?" she said.

"Not exactly," said Martijn. "No."

"Then what?"

"Your father's work revealed something that the Dutch government didn't really want to know. Something sensitive, that they didn't want him to share with the public."

Karin understood all of a sudden why her father had been so anxious for months before he was killed. How he couldn't sleep, and she would hear him wandering around in the living room in the middle of the night. Maybe why he'd been drinking all the time. He'd told her that he was going back to Syria and that he had to "make something right." Then he'd insisted on coming out here, to the forest, to photograph the mouflons one more time. It had seemed a little weird then—he hadn't even been trying to sell his nature photographs to *National Geographic* anymore. But it was time they could be together, and alone, and that was what made it special.

Maybe even then, she thought, he'd known that if he went back someone would try to kill him. Maybe even then he'd thought it was the last time he would be able to share with Karin. Maybe he had wanted to get out here to bury something—could that be? Could it be that this sharp-edged box she could feel with just the tips of her fingers, in the hollow at the base of this tree, was what he had hidden? What Martijn was looking for?

"He told you the photos were here?" Karin said.

"He said he buried them in a place he loved."

Karin thought this over. That was her father. She knew he was like that. He might say something like that, a kind of riddle.

She remembered what her father had told her that last day when they were here, in this park, on their last camping trip before he died. "Life gets too complicated sometimes," he'd said. "You think you're doing the right thing, but it turns out you're on the wrong side. And then you have to find your way back."

Karin looked at Martijn's face and saw that he was paler than pale. He was a ghost. She figured it out. He had followed her here because he believed that her father had already told her where he buried the photographs. He thought she would lead him to this place. He had planned this all along. He had come on this dropping with her to…to…get it back. And now they were here, and without trying to—she was pretty sure now—she had actually found what he was searching for.

It was all so creepy and terrifying. Who had he been all this time? Did he ever love her mother? Did he ever want to be her stepdad? Or had all of this been an act for the last few years? Was everything about him just completely phony?

"You didn't work for the government," she said. "You had him killed, didn't you? It was you."

His pale face glowed in the dark, and he shook his head slowly. Something about him no longer looked like he felt bad about anything, or like he was trying to convince her of something.

"Why? Why isn't anyone there at the campsite?" she asked. "I thought you said they were already tucked into their sleeping bags. Why isn't anyone there yet?"

CHAPTER 28

SEARCH PARTY

Police vehicles had assembled in the south parking lot of the Hoge Veluwe National Park, encircling the meth camp. The parents had been called; the Scout program had been informed; an Amber Alert had been sent out across the Netherlands, just in case. But the investigation was centered around the grimy, soiled, chemical-smelling, drug-cooking lab in the forest.

It was no longer the middle of the night—it was now nearing dawn. Calls to Martijn were all unanswered; Rutger still hadn't heard from Riekje, Lotte, or Margot. Every minute that passed, Grace knew, was another minute that threatened the life of her daughter. Whoever had been at this meth lab camp could have attacked all of them, could have put her, and the others, in the back of a van and sped off with them, maybe even to another country by now. Where had they gone, and who had taken them?

The police detective in charge, a tall man with a dour expression affixed to his chiseled, serious face, approached Grace and introduced himself. "I'm Detective Ricardo van Dijk, and we're going to get this situation under control as quickly as possible," he assured her. "To make it simple for you, I'm your point of contact. You can call me Dick. Anything you need, come to me. Anything you need to share, tell me. I'll keep you apprised of our progress every step of the way. I promise that we will do our utmost to resolve this and get your daughter back to you. I understand how scary it can be when children go missing. We need to act fast."

This Dick van Dijk didn't look anything like the Dick Van Dyke of Grace's youth, he of *Mary Poppins* and *Chitty Chitty Bang Bang*. This Ricardo had caramel-colored skin and striking, pale blue eyes, which she guessed suggested Dutch and Surinamese heritage. There was something Dick Van Dyke avuncular about him, though. He had a calm, comforting energy and seemed to be someone she could trust to handle things, in spite of the militaristic staccato of his speech.

He informed her that the other parents were on their way here. His men would sweep the area of the meth camp in search of useful clues as to the whereabouts of Karin and anyone else who had been staying in the vicinity. He said that other agents were being sent out to patrol the rest of the park.

While waiting for the cops to arrive, Grace and Maaike had already scoured every bit of ground around the tarp. They'd found Karin's black jeans and a blue sweatshirt, and a pair of her socks with giraffes on the side, covered in mud. That alone had been unnerving. At first, she'd been afraid that she would discover Karin's body somewhere in the mud, and her heart had raced and raced, but it seemed they had covered the entire area and there were no human bodies. Only lots of chemicals and plastic garbage.

"My suspicion is that your daughter was not here

long," Detective van Dijk said, confirming what she already suspected was true.

"Why do you think that?" asked Grace.

"All that's here is her backpack and its contents. My gut tells me she was robbed, not kidnapped, and that her backpack may have been stolen from her elsewhere, somewhere on the trail over there. I've sent some men to scour that area for clues."

He was trying to calm her, but the word "kidnapped" traveled up her spine like an electrical current and reverberated.

Grace and Maaike had also asked the other police officers several times if they could join the search, but Detective van Dijk had insisted that they remain with him to answer questions. "If there is a real danger in the woods, you both could be potential victims of it as well," he said. "It would be irresponsible of me to allow anyone else to get lost right now." He promised them that his team was doing everything they could to scour the park, but having "two women out there with a bunch of domesticated dogs is only going to complicate matters."

"But they had her here," said Grace. "The danger was these people in this camp, wasn't it?"

Detective van Dijk shook his head, remaining calm and considered. "Maybe she wasn't ever in contact with them at all," he said. "It's possible she left her backpack somewhere and they found it, or snatched it from her and brought it here." Her daughter's backpack stolen at random by meth addicts while she was hiking—this was, apparently, the optimistic scenario.

"And the blood on her shirt?"

"I'm not sure it's blood. Has an unusual chemical odor. If it is blood, it could also be someone else's," he said officiously. "Someone else may have been hurt and used the nearest available rag, a shirt that wouldn't fit anyone in the camp, to stanch the wound. Our men will put the shirt through forensic testing."

"Where are the people who were living here—the...the junkies or whatever they are? Where have they gone?"

"My sergeant is checking with park rangers and the organized crime division to see what surveillance of this area is available," he said. "Whatever they encounter, we will know about it quickly," he added.

"Organized crime division?" she said. "You mean they may have known that this meth camp was here already?"

"Unfortunately, this isn't the first time. Lots of meth labs are springing up in our parks lately. Maybe you've read about it in the papers. It doesn't take much to cook meth, so they make their pop-up kitchens everywhere. Most of the things you need are just household items. You've probably seen *Breaking Bad*? Big market for the stuff. We've disrupted labs on houseboats and cargo ships. Less so in national parks, but yes, it can happen. Lots of un-surveilled land. Usually they're here for no more than a few days before they're detected. Sometimes we don't know about them until they're gone, leaving all their garbage behind."

Grace took this in. Her mind was racing, and she was imagining other terrifying scenarios. That the junkies had fed meth to Karin or run off with her. That she was in some horrifying warehouse now, filled with international kingpins. That they were selling her into sex slavery, transporting her across borders. She felt Detective van Dijk's hand on her shoulder. As if reading her mind, he said, "It's best not to let the fear overtake you. We need you to stay sharp now so that we can use whatever information you may have to find her and get her back to you. Here's what I can tell you: the fact that the other kids and two supervisors are also missing is in fact a good sign, at least as far as your daughter is concerned. My gut tells me that something entirely different is happening here, that may not have anything to do with this place. I just don't know what yet."

At least this was a little bit of relief to Grace. She needed more reassurances. "Please tell me that we're going to find her," she said.

He looked at her directly, his blue eyes translucent and focused. "As Dutch police, we don't make those kinds of promises. But, Grace, I'm going to tell you that working with the Amber Alert in the Netherlands, we do boast a ninety-four percent success rate in finding lost kids within forty-eight hours. We're especially good at it when we get early leads like we did in this case. So thank you for coming forward so quickly."

"And the other six percent?" Grace wanted to know. "What happens to them?"

"Well, it's interesting," Detective van Dijk said, this time letting his eyes travel across the scenery. "The other six percent is most often a parent who makes off with their kid across international borders, to get them out of the reach of the other parent. We have a lot of that here, international child abduction. Sometimes it's in the middle of a contentious divorce. Sometimes parents do it without even knowing that it's illegal to run off with your kid to another country without the consent of the other parent. But usually they do know."

Grace felt herself flush, a sudden heat in her chest and face. A parental abduction—could that be...It immediately struck her, like a punch to the gut, that Martijn could actually have something to do with this. He was missing too, but, well, that didn't mean that he was also a victim. What if Detective van Dijk was right, that this meth camp had nothing to do with what had happened to Karin and the others?

"In most cases," Dick van Dijk continued, "it's the mothers who abduct the children, sometimes trying to get them out of the hands of bad husbands." He paused. "I guess we can rule out that scenario, since I'm standing here talking to you." He smiled ever so slightly, but the thought made her shiver.

Grace began to sweat inside her clothes. She unzipped her jacket and tugged at her collar. What he said made perfect sense. Wasn't that what they always said? The people closest to you are the most likely ones to do you harm?

At that moment another police officer approached and pulled Ricardo aside. "Excuse me," he said to Grace. "Detective, I need a private conference." And the two of them walked away from her, just as her head began to reel from all the other possibilities of what could have happened to Karin. Could Martijn have followed her here on purpose? For what reason? To abduct her? But to where?

The two men had walked to a spot under a tree where the branches nearly grazed their heads. Watching them, she started to consider what Detective van Dijk had said and how it connected to what she had learned about Martijn that morning. Was it possible—could it be—that these things weren't separate factors in her life, separate problems upending her existence, but one and the same? Could Martijn's issues at home be linked to the problem with this dropping?

Maaike, who had been standing some yards off this

whole time, trying to keep her dogs under control, lurched toward Grace on her booted foot as soon as she saw the police detectives move away. "Grace, did they give you any information?" she said softly. "Do they have any leads?"

Grace shook her head. "No, nothing yet," she started. "Karin has been missing for *hours,* and we are only now trying to find out where she is. We're so far behind. Maaike, I'm afraid, I'm terrified, and I don't know what to do. I want to tell you something, and I need you to tell me if I'm crazy. Tell me if I'm losing my mind."

Maaike nodded compassionately. "I'm sure this is all very upsetting," she said. "You're not losing your mind; you're just naturally upset."

"No, it's not that. It's that I'm afraid maybe my husband has something to do with this..." She didn't say out loud the other thoughts she was thinking. "If it's true, I'll never forgive myself. To put her in danger...The only important thing in the world to me is Karin, and I'm afraid my husband, her stepfather, may have been involved..."

"I don't understand," Maaike said, steadying herself on her foot in the mud and rubbing Grace on the back. "Why would he be involved?"

Suddenly there was the sound of a car arriving, and a man and a woman jumped out. Grace recognized them from the drop-off: Margot's parents. The mother was as thin as a praying mantis and the husband a stocky wrestler type, who walked directly to the police officers, demanding answers. "I want to know what has gone wrong here," he said. "I thought my daughter was going to have an adventure, and we were going to have a night off."

Detective van Dijk shook the father's hand and started to explain how the operation was working.

"Please, Bart, allow the officers to do their work," the mother implored. "Don't get in their way."

The detective told him that he was receiving a briefing, which might help them understand the situation better, and asked the dad to wait nearby if he could. With a huff, the father agreed.

"I told you we should have given her that watch with the GPS tracking device for her birthday," Margot's mother said, pulling him away from the officers. "She would have liked it and worn it all the time. It's also a digital watch. Then we'd just know where she is."

"She would have had to leave it at home for this trip anyway," he responded. "They weren't allowed to bring any digital technology at all."

"We could have also put one of those little GPS trackers in her shoes," she added, as if she hadn't registered his objection. "She wouldn't even have noticed that, and I bet that wasn't off-limits."

"Sanne, I object to the notion of tracking our daughter's movements like she's cattle," the father said decisively. "Childhood should be childhood. Nobody had to know where I was at every moment when I was a kid. We just got to run around free, like kids. Parents didn't go to pieces if we didn't show up at home immediately." Now he glanced in Grace's direction, nodding in acknowledgment, as if he hadn't seen her there before.

Maaike, who was still at Grace's side, volunteered help-fully, "We grew up in a different world, didn't we? It was so much freer and safer then. We were lucky."

Sanne responded to both Maaike and her husband, "Well, that's only because we just didn't know that all the priests were molesting children and all these pedophiles were out there selling kiddie porn and all that kind of thing. Who knows if kids were really safer? I think we were just ignorant of all the ways children could be put in danger."

The father sighed, exasperated, and walked off, announcing, "I'm going to see if I can find out anything."

"I'm sorry that my husband is taking this attitude," Sanne said to Grace and Maaike after he was out of earshot. "I think it's totally appropriate that you called the police. It's almost morning and the kids haven't been in touch with anyone for hours. I do hope it's nothing, though; I hope they are just fooling around, trying to frighten us all. And we can all go home soon and get some rest."

Then Grace's phone was ringing again. Grace saw that it was Rutger.

"Some progress," he said when she clicked on to the call. "Riekje found Lotte, and they are both here now, back at camp. Lotte has been hurt. She's got an injury to her head, and we don't know how she got it. But she's conscious and she was able to walk here with Riekje, and they are both safe now. Riekje had somehow lost her cell phone. That's why she didn't call. Lotte is getting looked at by one of the police officers who just showed up at the camp."

"Thank God," said Grace. "Did Lotte say anything about Karin?"

"She said she was with Karin after Dirk and Margot took off on their own; they were walking together and then she felt something hit her from behind. At first she thought it was Karin playing around, but then she turned around and didn't see Karin anywhere. She did see someone's feet. That's all she saw before she went unconscious, she said. Then she couldn't remember anything after that."

"Oh Jesus," said Grace. "Does she have a concussion?"

Margot's mother gasped on hearing this. Grace pulled the phone closer to her ear and cupped her hand over her mouth.

"Riekje is with her, and they are talking to the police now," continued Rutger. "An ambulance is on its way. I'm pretty sure they will take her to the hospital from here. She says that she is only feeling dizzy, which is a good sign. But she must have been unconscious for a while."

"Did she say anything else about the feet she saw? Were they Karin's?"

"No, no. She said it wasn't Karin. She said she thinks it was an adult's feet, not a child's."

"An adult's feet..." Grace pushed further. "Did she think it was a man or a woman?"

"I'll see if I can ask her," said Rutger. "I'm trying not to put pressure on her right now, because she's hurt, and I think the police will ask the questions, do the investigating. But I'll try to find out what I can find out. Look," he added, "we're three out of six now, which is a good sign. We'll find the others, I'm sure."

Grace's mind began to reel, and she walked away from Maaike and Margot's mother. She felt suddenly light-headed, as if she were standing on the edge of a cliff. In this heightened state, her brain started to try to pull all the strands of the narrative together, like a spider building a web in reverse. All the information she had gathered today started to connect: Martijn's aggression toward her, the documents she'd found in his office, Karin's shirt, Karin's disappearance. The fact that Martijn didn't answer his phone, after all this time, when all this was happening. She couldn't figure out how it all connected, but she knew it must. There were just too many parts that seemed to point somehow to the same thing.

"Wait," Grace said to Rutger. "Ask her, ask Lotte, if you can, if she can remember the color of the person's shoes. Were they bright blue hiking boots? Ask her: bright blue hiking boots?"

CHAPTER 29

THE BOX

"There may be somebody there. But I took care of most of them," said Martijn. "Margot and Dirk helped me out a bit by splitting off from the group early on. I only had to take care of Lotte."

"'Take care of'?" Karin asked. "What does that mean? Where is she? Did you hurt her? Is she dead?"

"Not dead," he said. "I'm pretty sure she's not dead."

"*Pretty* sure?" Karin started to breathe more shallowly. If he had her father killed ... if he was willing to hurt Lotte ... if he had ... "What did you do to Margot and Dirk?"

"I just had to make sure they were out of the way," Martijn said. "They made it quite easy for me. I caught them when they were out in the woods, doing things they weren't supposed to be doing. I just told Dirk that he'd better get going or else I would make sure their parents and the Scout leaders were well informed about their mis- behavior. He took off into the woods after that. Margot I had to deal with a little differently. But when I left her she was still breathing."

"Still *breathing*?" Karin felt like she was speaking to a complete alien. What had happened to her stepfather? Was everything that mattered to him in the world contained in this metal box?

Karin was absolutely sure now that what she felt behind her back, in the hole in the tree, in the hollow, was the box he wanted. It was very small, no bigger than the size of a cell phone. It probably didn't contain film negatives—no, it was either a small hard drive or just a memory stick. The tips of her fingers were touching it, of that she was sure. But what would happen if she told him? What would he do once he had it? Was he going to "take care of" her as well? She just couldn't imagine that he would simply let her go.

"What did you do to Margot?" she asked. "Is she hurt? What did you do to Lotte?"

"I didn't want to hurt anyone," he said, as if he were completely innocent. "I just needed to get you alone out here, that was all. There are a lot more lives at stake than just a few girls in the Netherlands. You have to understand that. There are hundreds of thousands of people being killed over there." Now he was making it sound like he was some kind of humanitarian. But Karin already knew that he was only trying to save his own skin.

Martijn's pocket lit up. He pulled out his phone, which was vibrating. It had probably been vibrating all evening, over and over again, and he had been ignoring it. Karin figured it had to be her mom calling. She wished she could somehow get the phone out of his hands. Martijn just looked at it, as it lit up his face, and didn't answer it. He looked at her.

"Let me talk to her," said Karin. "Let me tell her what you're looking for. Maybe she can help. I'm sure she knows better than me. You can tell her what you want and she can help us find it. She's good at that sort of thing. Then we can all make sure you're exonerated, just like you wanted, and we can all go home, no problem, all safely. We won't tell anyone what happened. We'll keep it to ourselves, in the family. We'll just keep it between us."

Martijn let the ringing die out and the phone went dark again. "I'm not ready to talk to her," he said. "I don't think we're going to find what I'm looking for, so now I have no more recourse. I have to end this and just escape."

"What do you mean, 'end this'?"

"I've already caused too much damage," he said. "There's no turning back at this point. So I have to go forward. That means I have to get away from here, and I have to just leave the country. The Dutch authorities will be chasing me."

The phone rang again. He picked it up and looked at it but still didn't answer it. "Let me talk to my mother," Karin said. "Please. Please, Martijn. I'll explain that we got lost in the forest and that you are helping me find my way back. I'll tell her that we're fine and that we're on our way to the campsite. And I'll say that nothing at all is wrong. We all just got lost."

Martijn looked at her, as if considering this idea. But the ringing ended again, and the phone went dark again. "I think you have a good head for this," he said. "You're smart. You probably got that kind of thinking from your dad. But unfortunately, if we don't find the photos, I can't go back. I'll be arrested and put on trial, and I'll face the highest penalties for treason. There's no going back now. It's over for me."

Karin was pretty sure this meant that he didn't care much about her life either. Would he try to kill her now? Or could he let her go? He had told her everything, confessed to her. That probably meant he couldn't let her go now.

She moved her fingers and tried to grasp the small box in the hollow of the tree. If she could get it, she would give it to him, because that was the only way he would stop. But she had to find a way to get it, and then get him to untie her first. If she gave it to him when she was still tied up, he would leave her there, or he would kill her. If she got him to untie her, at least she could try to make a run for it. She was faster than he was, and if she got out ahead of him she could get away—she knew that much, at least.

Martijn's phone was lighting up again, and he was looking at it again. Like maybe he'd answer this time. She prayed he would answer. Maybe her mom could talk some sense into him. Maybe at least she'd be able to use some kind of GPS thing to figure out where they were. Martijn stared at the phone, as if it would maybe talk to him without him answering it. It was at least enough of a distraction for Karin to have time to thrust her bound hands back and reach into the hollow for the box.

He didn't answer the phone, but he did start to pace. Up and down in front of her. Up and down. Every time he turned his back, her fingers went to work behind her. She pressed on the hard edge of the metal case. She pushed until it started to kind of jiggle. He walked up, then he walked away. And she tried again. She could feel it coming loose from the tree. She could feel something happening.

At last she felt it fall into her palm. Yes, it was some kind of metal case. Not very large. It could only really be a memory stick in there. That was fine, because she could grasp it in her hand right now, and in the darkness he wouldn't be able to see. She had to keep hold of it until he untied her, somehow, without letting him see it. But how?

"Listen, Martijn," Karin started. "I have been sitting

here trying to remember. What you said about him burying something 'in a place he loved'? And I think I may have figured it out. He loved this place, definitely. But he loved another place in this park too. When you said that he hid them before he left for Syria the last time, it made me think. After we camped here that time, we went to the other place. We saw the mouflons in the morning, but then he said we had to pack up and we went to the museum for breakfast. I think I know where he might have put them, if he was hiding something. I think I know the place that he loved."

"What?" He nearly leapt at her then. "You've been holding out on me this whole time?"

"No, no, I just figured it out," she said. "I just remembered that day and where we went. After we were here, at this campsite, we went to the museum. I thought it was weird that we went to the museum. He never did that. But I remember that we went walking in the sculpture garden. In the massive sculpture park outside the museum, and we stopped near a sculpture for a while..."

Martijn looked like he didn't really believe her. And that was normal, because she was lying. She wasn't a very good liar. But she had to get him to untie her. That was the first thing. Only he had to untie her without noticing the little box, which she was trying to slip into her back pocket. But it was hard because her hands were tied and she was sitting on her butt. Somehow she'd have to stand up again and get the box into her pocket without him noticing. She started pressing with her heels into the ground to try to push herself up to standing. As she did that, her arms scraped against the bark of the tree. It hurt a lot, but now she had hope.

"I'm going to lead you there," Karin said to Martijn. "I'll

show you which sculpture it's in. I don't remember the name of it or anything like that, but I will remember it when I see it. I'm sure that I'll be able to find it once I see it."

Little by little, she had gotten herself up to standing, at last. She was breathing pretty hard, and her hands were probably bleeding. "Just untie me, Martijn. Untie me and we'll go there together and find it and we'll get out of here. Look, it's almost morning. We'll call my mom and tell her we're fine. We'll figure out how to explain what happened with the other girls. You didn't really hurt either of them, right?"

Martijn paced again, giving her the moment she needed to drop the little box into her back pocket. He came to stand in front of her again. "I don't think so. I can find ways to explain what happened," he said.

As if he's some kind of mastermind, Karin thought. *But whatever. As long as he unties me.*

"This rope is hurting my hands," she had to remind him. "And I can't go anywhere until I'm freed."

He stared at her for a little while, probably trying to figure out if he could trust her. "Okay," he said at last. "I'll untie you, but you'll stay close to me, and lead the way." He added, "No strange moves."

"I know," said Karin. "I know. I'll take you right there. We'll get there before sunrise."

Martijn moved toward Karin and she did her best not to flinch as he grabbed her hands and undid the rope. She prayed that he didn't notice the bulge in her back pocket, and by some miracle it seemed he didn't. It was still just dark enough.

Once her hands were free, she shook them out; her wrists had been twisted in an awkward position and they hurt badly. She took a step away while still facing him, so he wouldn't see the box.

"We'll have to think of a really good story," she said. "But you're good at making up stories. I'm sure you can find a really good story for what happened to the other girls."

"Oh yeah," he said. "That's the least of my worries right now. Go on, Karin. Lead the way."

CHAPTER 30

PUZZLE PIECES

It all didn't add up to something in her mind yet, but Grace knew her suspicions were strong enough that she had to say something about it to Detective van Dijk. All that she suspected about Martijn—maybe it was crazy, maybe it didn't mean anything, but she had to tell him.

She approached the two police officers and tried to interrupt. But before she could speak, Detective van Dijk said, "Sergeant Vos just informed me that there was a police raid here last night, and the people who set up the meth lab were all arrested and taken into custody."

"My God. Was Karin with them?"

"No, and we have no reason to suspect that she had any presence here. No children were with them. Nor your husband or Riekje. The police team's investigator is questioning them now."

"Did they have any information about Karin?"

"What we know is that Karin is not with them," he repeated. "Neither Karin nor any of the other missing persons from the Scout camping trip. If she ever was with them, she left before the raid. The forensics lab also got back to us. It appears to be blood on the shirt, but it is not hers. One of the adults at the camp was injured."

"Thank God," said Grace. "Oh, thank God."

"But that still means she's somewhere out there," he said, dropping his voice to a lower register. "We were just looking in the wrong place, Grace."

Grace turned to look at the wide expanse of the forest. Thousands of acres of land. Woods and sand drifts and valleys and miles of heath. There were wolves, and maybe other predators. Why had they wasted so much time here when she was somewhere out there? It had to be Martijn, didn't it? Was it him, all this time?

Grace's phone pinged, with a message from Rutger: Lotte says YES to blue hiking boots. She remembers that. That was all I got. The EMTs have taken her to the hospital now. Her parents are meeting her there.

Grace's stomach sank. That confirmed it. Martijn.

She closed her eyes and saw all of it. The weeks, months, since they'd married and moved in together, all the ways he'd betrayed her trust. Since the first day the university student movers hauled her furniture and boxes into Martijn's house. His hands on her. His hands clenching her wrists, holding her down on the bed as she cried out. His shove, against the bannister, so hard she was sure she would fall down the stairs, and didn't only because he grabbed her again. His palm, smacking flat against her chest when she turned away from him during an argument, leaving an ugly bruise in the shape of a heart, of all things. And this morning's thrust against the kitchen cabinets. All that she had been denying to herself.

These weren't mishaps; they were cruelties. He said he

loved her, but this was how he treated her. Of course he would treat others this way too.

Grace turned immediately to Detective van Dijk. "I need to tell you something," she started. "I think my husband is involved."

The detective, surprised by this information, gave her a once-over, maybe trying to figure out if she had held something back from him before.

"You said that in these kinds of cases, it is most often someone close to the child who is responsible," she said. "Martijn. Karin's stepfather. He was supposed to be a supervisor on the trip, but I don't think he's lost. I think he's doing something...I don't know what or why...I haven't figured out what is going on, but I have good reason to believe that he is a dangerous man."

"Okay," Detective van Dijk answered. "I understand that you may have concerns, but let's figure out if this is real or just nerves. Sometimes, when we're afraid, our minds can play tricks on us. Let's find a place to sit down for a moment and talk privately." He added, "This way," guiding Grace to his car, which was not an official police vehicle but an unmarked Opel two-door. She let him open the door for her and she got in while he went around to the other side and got into the driver's seat. She understood why they needed this privacy—she was about to make a serious accusation.

"There's a lot to tell, but I don't want to waste any more time," said Grace. "My husband was wearing his bright blue hiking boots this morning. Rutger just told me that the last thing Lotte saw after she was hit on the head was bright blue boots."

"Okay, that's concerning and I understand the urgency,"

said the detective. "But it's not conclusive. Please tell me: What reason do you have to suspect that he may have become violent toward the children or kidnapped your daughter?"

She found herself trying to articulate what had happened. "This morning my husband and I had a fight. The altercation reached a pitch. He can be very...emotional." She was speaking a formal kind of language that sounded like police talk. "He became irrational, and I really didn't understand what he was so upset about. He seemed to be blaming me. I told him that I didn't know anything about what he was talking about. I suppose it was his frustration that made him turn aggressive."

"Aggressive. Did he hurt you?"

"I don't know if it was intentionally. He pushed me, very hard. I slammed against the kitchen cabinet and the door handle cut me." She reached a hand to the shoulder in question and pressed the bruise there lightly to confirm to herself that it really had happened.

"I'd like to have a doctor look at you later," the officer said calmly.

"We need to find Karin first," she said.

"Of course. Has your husband done this before?"

"This specifically, no. But he has"—she paused, finding it hard to say the words—"pushed me." Somehow she felt a need to clarify who he was to her. "Martijn is my second husband. My first husband was a photojournalist who was killed by a sniper in Syria."

Detective van Dijk was examining her face, registering everything she'd said.

"That was your husband?" he said finally, nodding. "I read about that."

An image of Karin, out there somewhere in the forest, in the company of Martijn, flashed through Grace's mind like an electric bolt. They were wasting time talking. What if he really had taken her? What if he had her right now?

"When he left on this Scout dropping, I went back to our house, where we live together, and into his office, and I started snooping around, trying to figure out what he was talking about. Whether there was something I was missing. I found strange things—files on my husband from long before I married Martijn. I don't understand what it all means, but I think it means there is something Martijn is looking for and maybe he now thinks Karin has it."

Detective van Dijk looked at her carefully, again in the eyes, and studied her face for the briefest of moments. "I've heard enough," he said. "I agree that we should not waste more time talking. He may be a suspect. Let's go forward that way. Have you spoken to him on the phone in the last few hours?"

"No," said Grace. "I've been calling and calling, but he hasn't answered. I spoke to him in the evening, once. After that, nothing. I thought this all had to do with the meth lab…I assumed whatever happened to Karin was the same that happened to him, to the others, but what if he has done something…what if he's not answering because—"

"Does he usually answer you right away when you call?"

"Mostly, yes. Unless he's turned off his phone."

"I understand you," said Detective van Dijk. "We're going to change our strategy now. I'm going to send the patrol cars out looking for him. But as you probably know, he could be anywhere. There are thirteen thousand acres of land in the forest."

"I want to go," said Grace. "I want to go with one of your patrols."

"It will take less time if we could narrow down his location, and to do that it will help if you stay with me. I need you to give me his cell phone number, and we will request a tracker from his phone service. But that takes time too."

"I understand. How can we make it go faster?"

"If you can manage to get him on the phone somehow, we could pinpoint his location with his GPS tracker. If you can get him talking, even for a minute, we'll know his exact location. But you have to get him to talk."

Grace felt frantic. How could she make him answer? "He doesn't pick up. That's the problem. I call, but he doesn't pick up."

Detective van Dijk thought about this for a moment. "Does he already know that you suspect him?"

"I don't know. Maybe. When I called him last night, I told him that I had found some files in his office. I may have tipped him off..."

"That could be why he's not answering your calls now," said Detective van Dijk. "Can you find a way to explain that away and let him think you are on good terms? That nothing is wrong? Would that work?"

"I could send him a text message. Maybe he'd read that?"

"That's worth a try. Have you already informed him that Karin is missing?"

"No, but I have been calling and calling. If he's looking at his phone at all he knows something is up."

"He may be pretending to be asleep. But anyway, that's good. That works to our advantage. Text him something normal and bland, about pickup times, or laundry or dinner reservations."

"It's before dawn. Why would I be contacting him this early?"

"Tell him you can't sleep because you miss having him in bed beside you," said Detective van Dijk. "It's worth a shot. If he believes you don't suspect him, he might be willing to talk."

There was a knock on the car window, and Grace looked up. It was Maaike.

"I'm going to return to my house now, get the dogs home," she said. "Your car is still at my house, so I can come back and pick you up later, when you're ready. You know how to reach me by phone, and you are always welcome to call if you need my support in the meantime."

Grace nodded.

"I want to hear as soon as you have your girl back," Maaike continued. "Okay? Make sure she's all right, catch your breath, and then call me."

Grace promised that she would.

"That moment will come sooner than you think," said Maaike, before tugging at the leash ring and hobbling away.

Grace watched as she piled the dogs into the back of her car, and then Grace took her phone in her hands. To Detective van Dijk, she said, "Just tell me what to say."

CHAPTER 31

TAKE CHASE

Martijn had forced Karin to walk in front of him, like a prisoner on a death march. She had to lead the way. And this made her particularly worried, because the little metal box was in her back pocket. She longed to take it out of that pocket and put it somewhere safer. All he had to do was shine his headlamp down on her backside, and he'd see it there.

They hadn't walked very far when Karin heard his telephone beep. He had a text message, and she knew it had to be from her mother. *Curiosity killed the cat*, thought Karin as she heard the shuffling of his feet stop behind her, and she turned around to look.

"Don't move," he said as he focused on the glowing screen. "Stay right where you are."

She did as he told her, but her hand moved slowly behind her back, and she managed to grab the box again and move it to the front pocket of her jacket. It would still be possible for him to find it there if he gave her a pat-down, but right now he had no reason to believe she had anything at all. That, at least, was lucky.

Karin watched Martijn read the text message her mom

had sent, and heard his cynical laugh. "Your mom must really think I'm dumb," he said, shining the screen in her direction. "She's trying to tell me that she misses me terribly now that I'm away for one night. And could I please call her because she's feeling..."

Before he finished his sentence, Karin sprang forward and swiped the phone out of his hands. He was faster than she thought he would be, and he managed to grab her arm as she was turning. But she yanked hard and pulled her arm loose. She could run, that much she knew. If she could get out ahead of him, she could run way faster than he could. She turned and tried to sprint. But he managed to stick out his leg and trip her. She fell to the ground but kept the phone in her hands. While he attempted to pull her back, she found the most recent call and pressed it. *Dial, dial.*

The phone rang—she could hear it ring—even as Martijn threw his whole body weight on top of her, trying to climb his way up to her hand, which she held outstretched in front of her on the ground. She elbowed him and wriggled under his weight. If only she could get out from under him, she could run. She could run and he would not be able to catch her. She could tell her mother where they were. But where were they?

Martijn would not let her stand up, though; he pressed his knee into her back and she cried out.

"Karin?" She could hear her mother's voice on the other end of the line. It was her mother, at long last. "Karin, are you okay?"

Martijn tried to wrestle the phone out of Karin's hand. She tossed the phone forward, ahead of her in the dirt, and she elbowed him in the jaw to try to get him off of her.

He crawled over her head and grabbed the phone, quickly putting it to his ear.

"Grace! Hey! It's me," he said. He was breathing heavily, but he was trying hard to sound normal. Karin knew her mother wouldn't buy it. "Sorry, dropped the phone."

Karin could not hear the words on the other end of the line. "Yeah, Karin twisted her ankle. It's pretty bad. She fell down, and she was alone in the woods. But I found her! She's all right. Just hurts every time she takes a step, as you can hear. We're still on our way to the campsite."

Karin was still lying facedown on the ground. Martijn had put his knee on her shoulder to pin her. "Mom! Mom!" she cried. "I'm not okay..." He pressed his hand down to cover her mouth, pressing her lips into her teeth and making her lip bleed. She could taste the copper flavor of the blood in her mouth. She tried to bite his hand, but he pressed harder.

She could hear just the vague sound of her mother's voice. Was she looking for her? Did she know Karin was in danger? She must know that she was missing from the dropping. They must all know, mustn't they?

The thought that her mother was trying to find her made Karin suddenly roar. With all the energy of her twelve-year-old body, she heaved herself up from under Martijn's knee and hand and shoved him over into the dirt. "Mom!" she cried. "Help me. He's got me. He won't let me go. He's looking for something, but he's holding me hostage. You have to send the police."

Martijn, in his fury, threw the phone at Karin and then lunged at her to try to make her stop shouting. She didn't stop. "I'm in the middle of the forest, near the mouflon place. Somewhere between there and the museum."

She kept yelling while she scrambled to find the phone in the dirt. She had no idea if her mother had heard what she'd said. Then she saw it, glowing there in a heap of grass, and grabbed it before Martijn could leap on her again.

Once she had it in her hand, she ran. She ran as fast as she could. Martijn was not far behind her, but she held the phone to her ear and spoke, "Mom?" she said. "Mom, are you there?"

"Karin! Thank God. I'm here. We're coming! We're going to get you. The police are here. Try to get somewhere safe. We will find you."

Karin kept running as fast as her legs would carry her. She could sense Martijn behind her, and he wasn't far. His breath was loud and labored as he ran—that was lucky for her; he was middle-aged and out of shape—but she could hear it just behind her back. She ran on, never losing speed, and starting to gain momentum when she got over the top of the mound and started down the incline toward the forest. She could see the line of dark evergreens so close, and she was going to make it.

Then Martijn's hand landed on the back of her shoulder and got hold of the neckline of her jacket and pulled it hard. She was jerked back and almost fell, feeling the collar of her zipped-up jacket tight against her neck, the zipper digging into her skin.

For a second, she thought the jacket would strangle her if she didn't fall, but she managed to reach up and grab the zipper and unzip the jacket, so that it came loose and fell off her back. Martijn toppled backward into the sand, holding the jacket in his hand, but not Karin. The phone flew out of her hand then too, and she couldn't turn around and get it. She could hear Martijn cursing as she tensed her legs and picked up speed. He had the box now, she thought. He had the box in the jacket, if he bothered to search it. He would find the phone too. But he didn't have her.

And there was the forest, right in front of her. She dove into its embrace, smelling the soft, cool peat, the welcoming scent of pine trees. This place she had fled earlier was now a safe haven. She didn't have the phone, but her mother knew she was in danger—and that was good.

She slowed just a little bit to try to catch her breath, knowing that Martijn had fallen and it would take him a moment to find the phone and come and chase her again. Her chest was heaving from sprinting, and she was drenched in sweat. Her walking was fast, though, ducking under branches and feeling leaves whip against her face, until she could start running again. Then she looked around and saw a tree that was wide enough for her to hide behind, and she scrambled over to it, hoping that Martijn was far enough behind her that he wouldn't get here for a while—maybe until the police got there—and at least the tree might conceal her if he did.

The last thing she had heard her mother say before the phone flew out of her hand was "I'm coming, Karin."

CHAPTER 32

MEMORY

By this time, it had become a circus in the parking lot. Cop cars, the Amber Alert team, the Scout program leaders, and broadcast news vans from the early morning news crews of the local and national TV stations were all clustered near the gates. The reporters had been instructed by the police to stay well away from the parents for now, but they were hovering, ready to pounce, microphones in hand and video cameras on shoulders, as soon as they got the word.

Grace had run back to Detective van Dijk's car when Karin had managed to get a call out to her, and Detective van Dijk sat beside her as she screamed into the phone, trying to hear her daughter. Karin had bravely managed to keep the line open just long enough for the location to be traced by the cooperating phone company. They knew where they were. They just had to go get them.

Even before the line went dead, Detective van Dijk had received the location from the trackers, then relayed that information to all units and called out the police helicopter from nearby Arnhem. Grace was still screaming when he put a hand on her arm to comfort her. "You did good," he said. "We're going to get her back now." And he put his car into gear.

The car rumbled across the gravel and then spun out a little as they reached the dirt road. Grace was a wreck. She could not believe that her suspicions had been confirmed— Martijn, her husband, the man she had married, had done all this. He had hurt her, he had hurt children, and now he had kidnapped Karin and maybe at this very moment was hurting her too. Her head felt like it was about to explode with fear. She sat at the edge of her seat as Detective van Dijk drove and just screamed, *"Faster! Faster!"*

She glanced behind the car just long enough to see that they were being followed. At least a half dozen news vans were behind them, getting ready to capture this whole thing as it unfolded. How could she have let this happen? What had she done?

Detective van Dijk swerved onto a narrow dirt road that went directly through the woods; it looked barely wide enough for a car. They crushed patches of heath and drove through sand, over hills, and just barely beneath trees. It had to be against the park rules to drive here, but she was grateful. He was leaving some of the news vans in the dust.

"We'll be there soon," he said. "Don't worry."

But she did worry. All she could do was worry. Every second that passed felt like an unbearable eternity. "I'll try to call him again," she said. "Try to convince him..."

She dialed Martijn's number, assuming he would not pick up, but he did. The phone rang just three times, and then he was there.

"Hello, Grace." She heard his voice, the voice she had spoken to so many times over the last few years, when he had been her closest confidant. He had always had a surprisingly gentle voice, soft and low and kind. Who was this man she had thought she knew? That she didn't know at all? "Thank you for calling. You helped me locate the phone."

Oh shit, she thought. "Where's Karin?"

"That's a good question," he said with a chilling level of calm. "I seem to have lost her. She seems to have gotten away."

Detective van Dijk looked over at her, silently nodding. "Keep him talking," he whispered.

"What is this all about, Martijn? I don't understand. Why would you hurt little girls? Why would you try to kidnap Karin?"

"Oh, I had no intention of kidnapping Karin," he said, still surprisingly calm. "I like Karin. I don't want to harm anyone. I think the other girls must be okay, aren't they?"

"Other girls? What did you do to them? Where are they?"

"I'm guessing they're lying down in the grass, having a little nap, after they got a bump on the head," he said, as if he were telling a fairy tale. "You know I don't hurt little girls, Grace. I'm not a violent person."

"You don't think so?"

"Okay, well, I hurt you this morning, and I'm sorry for that, but you know you make me so angry," he said. "You really provoke me. I didn't mean to push you."

Grace swallowed hard. She knew that arguing with him at this point would not help at all. "What did you do to Karin? Where is she now?"

"Like I said, I lost her. She was supposed to lead me to

the place where Pieter hid something from me, but we never got there. It's a pity, really," he added. "If she'd only helped me to find it, this would be all over right now. I would be gone, and she would be fine."

"What is it that you need to find, Martijn?" she asked.

That was when he hung up.

CHAPTER 33

HIDING

Karin's legs were starting to cramp because she had them pulled so close to her body, up against the tree. Was Martijn even chasing her now? She didn't know, and wasn't going to look back to find out.

Maybe he had found the little box in her jacket pocket by now and was satisfied. She should have told him she had it. She should have just given it to him. Maybe then he would've just left. She hoped, she prayed, that he was somewhere out there, far away from here, and not coming anywhere near the forest. Not coming to get her anymore.

She started to shiver again, but she didn't know if it was from the cold, because she had no jacket, or if she was just afraid. How long would it take her mother to get the police to come? How hard would it be for them to find her now? How long would she have to wait? And would Martijn get to her first?

There was a crunching sound in the woods—footsteps. At first she thought, prayed, it could be deer. Couldn't it? It could be animals. Even if it was the wolves again, she would be happy. But it sounded like a step and then a slide, a step and then a slide. Like a peg leg walking in wet leaves. Karin tucked herself into a tiny ball, trying to become as small as she could possibly be, and squeezed her eyes shut tight.

"Karin," she heard a quiet, soft, girlish voice whisper, not far from her. "Karin, it's me."

She turned and looked, her eyes searching the woods around her, but she couldn't see anything.

Then it came again: "Karin, it's me. Look to your left."

Karin turned and saw Margot there, or at least her small face, swaddled in a green camouflage tarp that cloaked her inside a large bush. Her face was very dirty—almost half of it was covered in something black that seemed to coat her temples and cheeks. Her eyes were bloodshot; it seemed she'd aged ten years since Karin had seen her last, just yesterday.

"Margot," Karin whispered, but too loudly, knowing that she was endangering them both. She loosened her grip on her knees and crawled out from behind her tree and toward Margot's hiding place. They grasped each other in a hug, careful not to make too much noise. "How long have you been here?" Karin asked.

"I was just over there," Margot said, pointing to another clump of bushes. "I heard you run into the forest and I was afraid it was him, coming back. Then I saw it was you. I stayed quiet for a while until I saw that he hadn't followed you. It's been about fifteen minutes now, I think. I'm guessing that he's lost your trail or he gave up looking."

"What happened to your face?" Karin asked, reaching out to touch her fellow Scout, who just several hours ago she had disliked for no apparent reason. Margot drew back, not wanting to be touched.

"He hit me," she said. "It had to be him. I was walking along next to him and suddenly I felt this thing, like I'd been shot in the head, and then I fell. I think he used a rock, but I don't know."

Karin looked closer and understood that the black on her face was actually dried blood. "Oh my God..." Karin said, in the softest whisper she could manage. "You must have bled a lot. I can't believe he did that. I mean I *can* believe. I mean, he tied me up and chased me too. I think he's actually crazy."

"Wait a second," Margot said. "Shhhh." They both stopped their whispering and listened. Karin could hear the faint sound of something shuddering. Maybe it was thunder—a storm approaching. Maybe it was the rattling of a truck? The sound seemed to be repetitive and rumbling.

The two girls huddled together, and Margot opened her rain tarp to let Karin get in. She kept listening. It wasn't a sound of someone walking in their direction. It was coming from somewhere else entirely. It was coming from the sky.

It became clearer, and came closer. *Chud, chud, chud.*

It wasn't a storm, and it wasn't a truck. It was, Karin realized with a sudden burst of joy and relief, a helicopter! A helicopter was whirring overhead. Her mother, the police, whoever was going to save them, were on their way.

She looked up through the trees but couldn't see anything. But the more they listened, the more she was sure it was there. It was flying over the park. Soon it would be right above them. Whoever was inside the helicopter would be looking down, trying to find her. Trying to find them. They could be rescued!

But then she and Margot realized, maybe at exactly the same moment, that they probably couldn't be seen here, in the middle of the forest, with all these trees covering them. One of them would have to go back out into the clearing to get the helicopter's attention. Martijn would probably still be there. He'd be waiting for her, the moment she ran out.

She considered for no more than a few seconds and decided it had to be her. Margot was badly hurt, and it was her stepfather who had done it. She had to take the risk that he would see her, so the helicopter people would find them both. "I'm going," she said to Margot. "You stay here." Once she was on her feet, she added, "We'll get you once we've got Martijn in cuffs."

Margot yelled her name to try to stop her as Karin ran back in the direction she had come from, not sure how dense the forest was in any other direction. She kept her head up, eyes alert, as she tried to find her way out of the woods again. The whirring of the copter overhead drove her on, toward the end of the tree cover. *Chud, chud, chud.* It might not be long before they would see her.

Karin reached the edge of the trees and looked out, trying to see if she could spot Martijn, but the clearing seemed to be empty. She looked up and could see the helicopter had already passed and was going in another direction. It was about to be too far out of sight. Now was the time to go, if ever there was a time.

She threw herself into the open space and sprinted, right back up a large mound of heath where she knew she'd be visible to anyone who was looking—even Martijn. She started jumping up and down, up and down, waving her arms wildly. "Look here!" she shouted. "I'm here. Look here! Look here!"

Within seconds he was upon her. Martijn, seemingly out of nowhere, dove at her legs and knocked her down flat on the ground. All the air rushed out of her lungs when she hit the sand. It felt like she had been punched in the back. She couldn't inhale and she couldn't exhale for a few terrifying moments.

He climbed on top of her and tried to hold her down. His feet dug into her ankles and his hands pressed into her hands. He was heavy, and strong. Much stronger than she was. Karin struggled to breathe, wheezing through her chest.

Karin looked up and saw the helicopter, which seemed to be flying away, past the clearing. It hadn't seen her. They hadn't seen her. They were not coming back. And Martijn had her again.

Karin closed her eyes and tried as hard as she could to breathe. She had so little energy left. Finally, she managed to get some words out. "The box," she said. "You can have the box. It's in my jacket pocket. You can have it…" He was pressing her down into the sand and she could feel the ground starting to engulf her.

"What?" he said. "Where?"

"In my jacket pocket," she said. "You tore it off me. It's there, I swear. Go look."

Miraculously, he got off of her and went to look for her jacket. Maybe he knew where he'd left it, maybe he didn't. It gave her at least a few seconds to get her breath back. She could maybe use that moment to run off again. But she just wanted the helicopter to see her, and save her. "Please!" she cried, turning over and managing to get up onto her knees. "Please! Come back! Don't leave!"

Just then she heard a scream, loud and piercing, and a thump. She turned and looked where the scream had come from. She watched as Martijn fell to the ground—and behind him, there was Margot. She held a very large rock in her hand. She had somehow managed to hit him on the head with it.

Karin and Margot stared at him as he fell. Then Karin finally got a good look at Margot, because the sun had started to rise. One side of her face was covered in the dried black blood, and she guessed there was a big gash at the temple; a dark purple bruise had started to form near that eye.

Still holding a very large rock in her hand, Margot moved forward, so that she could stand over Martijn, where he had fallen. She held the rock up over his head and stood there menacingly, in case he tried to move again. Karin walked toward them, determined to keep him down if he tried to get up again.

The two girls stood over him as he put a hand to his temple and rolled over and his eyes blinked open. They could hear the *chud, chud, chud* of the helicopter again, which seemed now to be turning around, over the forest, and heading back in their direction, at last. Karin looked up to see the copter moving slower, and she waved her arms frantically. Margot also started jumping up and down, waving her arms and holding the rock in the air. "Here!" they cried, "Here!" until long after it was clear they didn't need to do it anymore. Karin started to breathe normally again as her hair began to whip in the wind. She felt relief, seeing the copter descend.

Martijn looked up at the girls, a trickle of blood falling from his forehead toward his eyebrows. He almost raised a hand to wipe it away. Margot raised the rock even higher. "Don't you even try it," she said. "Don't you even *think* about moving."

CHAPTER 34

ARRIVAL

Bands of deep pink and pale yellow spread like ribbons across the tops of the trees as Detective van Dijk's sedan finally slowed. Grace could see that the helicopter was already descending, while the detective's police radio started buzzing and pinging. "We've got eyes on some figures in the park," she heard someone say through the static of the machine. "Landing. Over."

Detective van Dijk grabbed the radio off his belt and spoke into it. "I've got eyes on you. We'll meet you in the clearing. Over." They could see it all happening in front of them. There in the distance. Karin was standing on a hilltop, with her back to them, and beside her was Margot. Grace could see Margot drop a very large rock from her hand to the ground, and the two girls embraced. They held on to each other tightly as the helicopter descended, whipping the sand and their hair up around them, so they seemed like they were standing in the midst of a typhoon.

Revving the engine so that he could drive up through the heath, the detective made eye contact with Grace, maybe to remind her that he was breaking all the park's driving rules to get her there as fast as he could. Then, when the sedan wouldn't drive any farther, he put it in neutral and nodded to her so she could jump out.

Grace opened the car door and starting running toward Karin before her feet even hit the ground. As she mounted the hill, she saw that a third figure was there, below them, lying immobilized in the sand. It had to be Martijn, who was seeming defeated. These two little girls had somehow taken him down on their own, and they were standing over him, and he was either unconscious or dead. As much as she wished him dead now, she hoped, for Karin's sake, that he was merely incapacitated. She felt a surge of pride in her chest as she ran higher, toward her daughter.

"Karin! Karin!" Grace was shouting, and that old response came to her call:

"Mom! Mom!" Karin cried out, turning and seeing her mother. Then she was leaping across the sand dunes, running down the hill and away from the helicopter, until she had reached her mother.

Grace held out her arms and Karin plunged into them, pressing her head against her mother's chest. Holding each other, they both began to weep. "I love you, I love you, I love you," Grace said, over and over, as she held Karin as close as she could, feeling the soft curve of her small back, touching her hair, stroking her neck. She stopped and pushed Karin away to look her daughter in the eyes. "I'm so sorry, I'm so sorry, Karin," she was saying. "I didn't know he was like this. I figured it out too late." She kissed her repeatedly on the face.

Even though Karin's eyes were red and wet with tears, she looked all right. She looked okay. "It's okay, Mom. It wasn't your fault," Karin said. "I'm okay. I'm all right. I'm not hurt. We stopped him!"

Now they were clutching each other again and crying. "I love you so much, I love you so much," Grace was saying. "I'm so sorry, I'm so sorry. I just wish you didn't have to go through this. It was so terrible. I should not have let you go alone. I have been trying to find you for hours..."

"I love you, Mom," said Karin. "It was Martijn. It was Martijn. It was all him."

There was a great deal of movement around them. The helicopter roared as it landed and sprayed sand all over the place. They covered their eyes and held each other against the wind. At the same time, they could hear the sound of an ambulance and police sirens in the distance. The cavalry was arriving. The reporters would be clambering up the hill soon.

Grace pulled Karin closer and spoke into her ear. "Did he do anything to you? Did he touch you? Did he—"

"No, he hurt Margot, but not me. He hit her on the head with a rock. He tied me to a tree and tried to get me to tell him something that Dad told me. But I didn't know what he was talking about. He said he was looking for some photographs. I don't know why."

As she said this, Karin realized that the metal box was still in her jacket pocket. But where was her jacket? She needed to find it—before everyone got there and took her away. "Mom," she said, "I need you to help me. We need to find my jacket—it has the photographs in them. It's somewhere here, I'm sure. Somewhere right around here."

Detective van Dijk approached and introduced himself to Karin, who immediately hugged him. "You helped my mom find me," she said.

He nodded, with humility. "Your mom did the hard part," he shouted above the din. "I'm going to need to talk to you shortly," he added. "Ask you some questions. But first I need to deal with your stepfather. You'll excuse me."

"Karin thinks there is important evidence somewhere here," Grace said. "We need to find it before we go anywhere. It's in her jacket, which she says is somewhere around here."

The detective said he would instruct some of the other officers to help them search for it. Police officers were already surrounding Martijn, lifting him to his feet and putting him into handcuffs. The helicopter had finally landed, and more vehicles were parking at the base of the hill.

Karin took her mother's hand and they began looking through the grass to try to find the jacket. "Why did he do it, Mom? Do you know why?"

"I don't know, Karin. I wish I knew. I don't understand what he wanted," she said. "It's a puzzle with a lot of missing pieces. But I guess you know a little bit and I know a little bit, and perhaps together we can figure it out. Karin," she added, stopping to look her daughter in the eyes. "I want you to understand that I didn't know until yesterday that he was dangerous. Maybe I had a feeling, somehow, but I kept hoping it wasn't true. I finally figured it out, but by then you were already in danger. I just want you to know that I never, ever, ever wanted that to happen."

Karin began to cry. "But, Mom, he's been hurting you," she said. "He's been hurting you since we moved in together. Don't you think that hurt me?"

"Oh God," said Grace. "I thought you didn't know. I thought it was only me. I didn't think . . . I just didn't want it to be true. I didn't want to admit it, even to myself. But it's true. And it's over now. It's over. He won't be able to hurt you anymore. I promise."

"Or you." Karin looked her mother sternly in the eyes. "Or you, Mom. I need you to be okay too."

"Yes, of course. He's going to be out of both of our lives. We'll make sure that he is put away, far away. And we will start over."

An ambulance had parked at the bottom of the hill, and now there were more people in uniform climbing up the sand dunes toward them. They'd take over from here. They'd want to ask questions. They'd want to see Karin, get her to a hospital. That was what was next.

They needed to find that jacket first.

Grace looked up to notice Detective van Dijk standing not far off from where they were, holding on to Margot, talking to her. He had a mild look of satisfaction on his face, just barely recognizable, and Grace felt again a pang of gratitude toward this man who had helped her get her daughter back.

Karin pulled away—not far, but it suddenly sent Grace's heart racing again—and she pointed to a spot in the grass. "I see it," she said. "My jacket is right over there." She ran to it, picked it up and dusted the sand off, and then slipped her hand into the pocket. She pulled out a small metal box, and held it up in the air.

CHAPTER 35

AFTERMATH

Grace and Karin sat together on a wooden bench in the wide marble-floored hallway of the International Criminal Courthouse in The Hague, their hands clasped together in a shared prayer. On either side of them were Jenny and Maaike, who had stayed in touch since the dropping.

Ten months had passed since that frightening night, and the two of them were back in The Hague for the first time since they had stayed with Jenny in late October last year. It seemed like ages ago, and then again it seemed like it was just yesterday.

They had survived, recovered to a certain extent, and gone back to their lives—though they were new lives, not the old ones. They had moved out of Martijn's house and into an apartment of their own in Amsterdam, and they had gotten a dog—a big cuddly Great Dane. Jasper and Frank had gone to live with their mom, and Martijn had gone to jail.

In spite of everything that had happened, Karin had insisted on continuing with the Scouts and was going on another dropping this summer, because she reasoned that she would have had a good time if Martijn hadn't "ruined everything." She finally wanted to have the dropping she had planned for. Anyway, she said, she wanted to work her way up to being one of the program leaders, later. She still believed that people could learn a lot from putting themselves out in nature.

While they tried to live their private lives, they sometimes saw what had happened to them, and how other people saw it, by watching the news. Their story had been shown pretty much everywhere, with the dramatic helicopter rescue captured by the news crews that morning as the main clip. That was funny because actually the helicopter had flown off without them, and they'd just gone in the ambulance to the hospital.

All three girls had been quite shaken up, but they weren't badly injured. With the cut on Margot's head, her sleep had to be monitored for a few days, but she was okay in the end. Martijn had hit both Lotte and Margot with a rock—probably the same rock—but aside from that, they were unscathed. He had only wanted to get Karin alone, it seemed, and that's what he had succeeded in doing.

Grace and Karin had arrived at the court very early that morning, two hours before the hearing was supposed to start, in order to get inside the big mirrored-glass building before the news vans arrived, blocking the doors and bombarding them with questions. They were pretty used to that kind of treatment by now. They'd been through this a few times already, first after Pieter's death abroad and then repeatedly since the dropping, so they knew a few strategies for getting away from reporters. But now, via their phones, they could watch as the news started running updates from somewhere outside this enormous building.

There was a sound of clacking on the marble—sturdy high heels moving down the nearly empty corridor—and they both glanced up to see Lily Oppenbauers approaching. Ms. Oppenbauers, all six foot two of her, was the public prosecutor for the case against Martijn. She was a strikingly thin woman with a narrow face and high, angular cheekbones who looked like a fit model for the skirted suit she was wearing. Grace had once joked to Karin that they could precast her in the role of herself in the movie version of their story.

They had been doing that a lot lately—casting people in the movie they imagined being made about their lives. It seemed to be a useful coping mechanism that helped them both process the whole horrible experience. They had already cast Kristen Stewart as Karin and Sophia Loren in the role of Grace—it was all a fictional exercise, so it didn't matter if the casting made any sense—although Grace guessed a better choice as mom would probably be Pamela Adlon.

Looking at Ms. Oppenbauers, though, Karin didn't laugh. She just gazed up aghast, with a dropped jaw, like she was seeing a giant. Well, teenage girls needed strong women to look up to these days, thought Grace, and some of them should look really good.

"Good morning, ladies," Ms. Oppenbauers said in English, with a comically thick Dutch accent, arriving in front of them at their bench. "How are you both feeling today? Are you ready to *kijk sam ass*?" She was trying her best to sound like someone out of an American television show, but it came out rather hilarious. They all laughed.

"I'm ready," Karin volunteered. "I'm ready to kick some, er, arse...," she said, glancing at her mother to be sure *this* curse, in this case, was allowed.

Grace had no role in today's proceedings, but Karin had one. This was the first of two cases Martijn was going to have to face—the "attack in the Veluwe," as they were calling it, was a local criminal case, and the larger case in the International Criminal Court about his role in the Syrian Salafist group scandal. That one centered on the photographs Pieter had taken—the ones on the memory stick in the little box Karin had managed to retrieve in the Veluwe. How strange it was, the way life worked out.

Karin and Grace had tried to piece together what happened to Martijn in Syria, but neither of them had understood the full story. Once the photographs were released, however, it all became very clear very quickly. What they showed was Martijn in the company of Salafi jihadist rebels in Syria, a crucial bit of evidence in a case claiming he had been collaborating with the jihadist group, a betrayal of Dutch government mandates.

Martijn had not hired Pieter to take photographs, it turned out. Pieter had discovered what was going on and had managed to document it. He had been planning to publish the photographs and expose Martijn as the liaison for the group—a group Martijn had convinced the Dutch government to support. Martijn had found out just in time and stopped Pieter from taking the images to the news agencies by paying him off. Pieter had agreed to the deal, apparently unable to say no to the money—but he had also insisted that if he died, the payout would be made to his widow and daughter. Did Pieter worry that, after what he'd uncovered, the rebels would have him killed anyway? Grace still didn't know the answer to that question.

But finally, that at least provided Grace with an explanation for the money they had received through Martijn after Pieter's death. The fact that Pieter had been willing to take a bribe and withhold important evidence of an international scandal seemed...well, unlike Pieter. But Grace knew he'd faced a difficult choice. Maybe she would find out more information about him—as Martijn had evidently tried to do—by looking into his old files, going back to the days in South Africa.

Grace would have to reconcile this new image of her first husband with the one she had built up around him since his death, but at least it helped her think of him as a fallible human rather than a martyr. Thinking of him that way would be good for Karin too, for whom all of this was much harder and would involve many conversations, she guessed, over many years. Their lives would never be simple or easy.

Anyway, it seemed that Martijn's accounting firm had always been a front for his illegal operations. He'd indeed inherited it from his father, but he barely did real financial work there. Still, it had come in handy when he needed to give Grace the payout.

Although she had refused contact with him after his arrest in the Veluwe, Martijn had written Grace a letter. In it, he had tried to explain what happened to him. He wrote, "You may think now that everything between us was a lie, but it wasn't. From the moment I met you at Pieter's memorial service, I was already in love with you. When you came to my office that first time, I told myself not to get involved, but I realized how much I had done to destroy your world, and I wanted to help. At first, it was that. And then I just wanted you to be my wife. I wanted to make things better for you."

But as their lives progressed, he had realized the walls were caving in on him. Some other reporters had been sniffing around the situation in Syria and the government's support of the Salafists. And maybe Martijn had started to worry that Pieter somehow had gotten the photographs out, in spite of the payoff and the secrecy. He had tried to find out what he could about Pieter, but he couldn't find all of what he needed to know. He became convinced that he had to destroy the photos to be safe and to be able to escape prosecution.

"It was my stress," he wrote to Grace, "that made me turn angry and aggressive. I never wanted to hurt you or Karin—that was never my intention."

What did it matter now? thought Grace. It didn't matter. She just wanted to try to forget everything that had happened and move on with her life. Her recovery was a small part of it, but her focus now was on Karin. She'd lost her father to violence, and she'd been a victim of an assault by her stepfather. How would she ever trust men again? What could Grace do to help her daughter go out into the world without feeling terrified or suspicious? These were the things they had to work through now. They had counselors, they had friends, they had a lot of attention from all kinds of professionals, if they wanted it. But for the moment, they first had to get through this.

Grace had done her best to keep her daughter out of the media storm so Karin could recover emotionally, get on with school, and try to find her way back to a normal life. This was the first time they would see Martijn in person, hopefully just briefly, since the dropping. Karin, although scared to death of this moment, had also been looking forward to it as a time when she could take the power back into her hands. That was important. Her mother, still holding Karin's hand, gave it a hard squeeze.

Ms. Oppenbauers had instructed her in what to do. All

that was expected of her today was to explain how she had found in the woods the box that contained the memory stick. Well, of course, it wasn't all that simple. But the evidence she had provided to the court was essential to the prosecution. And she had to answer a few questions about how she had obtained it. Martijn would be in the court-room, but Grace had told her that she didn't have to look at him, didn't have to point him out, didn't have to interact with him at all. Karin understood.

Grace hadn't always been viewed favorably by the pros-ecutorial team. At first, Ms. Oppenbauers had her held and questioned as a possible accomplice, because the link between her first husband and her second had been strong. It was hard for them to understand why she hadn't known about it. But it didn't take long for the prosecutor's office to believe her, especially after Detective van Dijk explained how the events in the park had unfolded. She had also promised to share everything she had with them—which she soon discovered was quite a lot.

This was part of her recovery too, said her new therapist. It was time she stopped beating herself up about "not knowing more at the time" or "not seeing people for who they really are" or "being blind to what was happening all around her"—all the ways she blamed herself for what had happened. By working with the prosecution and learning as much as she could about the situation in Syria, she could heal. If it was ignorance that had made her a victim, it would be knowledge that would help her recover.

Karin, meanwhile, was doing much better, thanks in part to months of therapy and to some new crucial friendships with Margot and Lotte. She still went once a week to see a woman who specialized in traumatic stress experiences, but she wasn't crying as often lately, and she had gotten back into a rhythm at school. Her grades had gone back up. The fact that her mom was so involved in actively making sure Martijn got his comeuppance seemed important to that recovery, Grace thought.

In the wake of all this, in addition to her job at the NGO, Grace was writing a book using Pieter's Syria photographs. The photos that had not been published because of Martijn's intervention were only a small part of the work he had done there. It turned out there were many more important photographs on that memory stick. There were also the photographs he had taken of the 2012 battle of Damascus and the destruction of the temple there, his insider's look at the torture hospital, and his images of ordinary life under the siege. Pieter had had his failings, but he had done quite a lot of revelatory work in Syria. Grace wasn't glossing over the complications of his ethics; in fact, that was what made the book of particular interest to her. People weren't perfect, and Grace had had to teach her daughter that too.

"I think we're just about to go in," said Lily Oppenbauers. "We'll take a seat in there and wait till the rest of the prosecution team arrives."

They were all rising to follow Ms. Oppenbauers when Karin saw Margot step out of the elevator down the hall. She ran toward her, and the two hugged. Grace had not expected Margot to be here for this—she didn't have to come—but the two girls had become very tight since the dropping.

Margot still had a small crescent of a scar on her temple where Martijn had hit her, but Grace thought it might fade over time. She'd had to have ten stitches when she arrived at the hospital, but she had been in such good spirits—it was remarkable. Margot had said that the whole experience had somehow made her feel powerful, in spite of how scary it had been. Grace watched as Karin and Margot walked down the hall together arm in arm, with Margot's parents behind them, giving Grace a vague, friendly smile.

The doors to the courtroom opened and then more people started to arrive and file inside. Grace waited before the doors, her heart swelling with gratitude that this moment had finally come. She needed to take a deep breath before she saw Martijn again.

Just before she walked into the courtroom to join everyone else, she glanced over her shoulder and saw another familiar figure walking toward her, with his calm, confident way, and his translucent blue eyes: Detective van Dijk. He didn't need to be here today either. This wasn't his case.

Grace mused for a moment how this terrible incident, which had exploded the family she thought she'd been building, in some ways had led her to find a new community of people who supported her and surrounded her. She was back in touch with Jenny. She had met Maaike, who had become something of an adopted grandmother figure for Karin. They had become close to all the kids from the Scout group—Dirk, Lotte, and Margot—and their parents. And even though she had often thought about leaving this country that wasn't her home and heading back to the US to raise Karin in that familiar place, she now felt she couldn't leave. There was too much holding her here.

"How are you feeling today, Grace?" Detective van Dijk asked her as he arrived at the door, took it from her, and motioned her inside.

She smiled. "I feel all right," she said. "For the first time in a very long time, I feel all right."

ABOUT THE AUTHOR

Nina Siegal is an American novelist and journalist who's lived in Amsterdam for fifteen years. She has previously published two novels (the first a literary mystery), and she is a regular contributor to the *New York Times,* covering European culture. She also writes and edits for many other international publications. Born in New York City and raised in the city and on Long Island, she graduated from Cornell University with a BA in English literature and received her MFA in fiction from the Iowa Writers' Workshop. She lives with her eight-year-old daughter, Sonia, who was born and raised in Amsterdam, and their dog, Coco.

MULHOLLAND BOOKS

You won't be able to put down these Mulholland books.

TROUBLED BLOOD *by Robert Galbraith*

THE BOOK OF LAMPS AND BANNERS *by Elizabeth Hand*

BLOOD GROVE *by Walter Mosley*

SMOKE *by Joe Ide*

LIGHTSEEKERS *by Femi Kayode*

YOU'LL THANK ME FOR THIS *by Nina Siegal*

HEAVEN'S A LIE *by Wallace Stroby*

A MAN NAMED DOLL *by Jonathan Ames*

THE OTHERS *by Sarah Blau*

Visit mulhollandbooks.com for
your daily suspense fix.